THIRTEEN

ALSO BY SHANI STRUTHERS

A Psychic Surveys
Companion Novella

THIRTEEN

SHANI STRUTHERS

STORY
LAND
PRESS

Dedication

For Misty and Isabella Skye.

Acknowledgements

I've visited the misty Isle of Skye many times. I've even named my daughters after it (see the *Dedication*) and earlier this year, for a special birthday, I visited again. It was indeed a wonderful trip, and from it, the idea of this book was born – it offers the perfect backdrop to Ness's troubled story. Minch Point Lighthouse is based on Neist Point Lighthouse, which sits abandoned and lonely, on Skye's most westerly tip. I visited on a sunny day, but it'd be amazing in fierce weather too, the atmosphere like nowhere else I've ever been. So a big thank you to Skye, to the lady who said I 'must' visit the lighthouse, and the magic that's still there in abundance. Thank you also to my beta readers – Rob, Louisa, Lesley and Vee, to Gina Dickerson for another great cover and Jeff Gardiner for his editing. Thanks also to the Psychic Surveys characters who've come alive in my head and won't let go. I hope you enjoy this latest journey.

Prologue

1972

"GO away, let me sleep."

The hand tugged at my bed sheets.

"I told you to stop it! Leave me alone."

But, Ness, it's snowing. Come over to the window and see.

"You said it was snowing an hour ago and it wasn't."

I said I thought it was going to snow, but now it is, it really is.

"So what," I responded, unable to help the petulance in my voice.

Don't you like snow?

Of course I liked snow, what child didn't? What I didn't like was being teased, and she was teasing me, she definitely was. She *always* teased me.

You're no fun, do you know that, Vanessa Patterson?

"And you're annoying, do *you* know that?"

You're lucky to have snow in your world, to be able to go out and play in it.

"Play in it? It's nearly midnight!" As if Mum would let me go and play at this time.

I can go though. She's got no control over me.

"No one's got any control over you."

She laughed, a tinkling sound, mischievous.

You're jealous really, aren't you?

"Of you? No."

You are, because Mum can't touch me, she can't hurt me.

"I said I want you to go away!"

You should stand up to her, be a little braver.

"Don't tell me what to do."

You should tell her about me.

Incensed by her words, I sat up, any attempt to sleep shoved to one side. "How can I tell her about you?" I hissed. "You know what she's like."

Again she laughed. *I know exactly what she's like.*

"Then don't be so daft."

The shape, the figure, my twin – my *dead* twin – left me and drifted over to the window, where she tugged the curtain aside. It amazed me she could do that, that she could actually touch things, interact – someone, *something* like her. She had no substance, was barely an outline at times, part of the spiritual world, not material, so how was it possible?

I told you it was snowing.

Unable to resist, I peered beyond her and into the night. She was right. It was! It really was. She hadn't been teasing after all. Big fat glorious snowflakes were pirouetting past my window, offering such a contrast to the darkness of the sky.

I leapt from bed and ran over to the window too – thick snow was covering the ground, the shed, the hedges and the tops of the garden walls.

You want to go outside, don't you?

I did. I longed to.

Even at this hour?

"Even at this hour."

Mum will be asleep.

"What about Dad?"

Him too.

And my brothers and sisters, would they be asleep too? I had five siblings – five that were living that is – the two older girls shared a room, so did the three boys. It was just me in a room on my own, and I say alone, but more often than not I wasn't.

Come on, get your shoes on and come with me.

I'd need my shoes, my coat, my hat, my gloves and scarf, and then I'd need to tiptoe down the stairs as silently as my twin; I'd need to *glide*.

She was right about me. I *was* jealous sometimes. I wanted to move around like she did; I wanted to hide, to disappear at times, to boldly face the disapproving glare of my mother, to shrug off the stifled laughter and nudges of my siblings. I was the youngest of the six children; that is, *we* were – my twin and I. I was also different from them, although I was learning to keep those differences to myself. I had to for survival's sake. My twin had asked me to tell Mum about her, but I'd tried once, she knows that full well. I'd said to Mum that my sister was still with us and that I saw and spoke to her often. I don't want to think about what happened next; how hard I was beaten, whilst my twin looked dolefully on. She was denied, just as I was – both of us feeling like outcasts.

Ness, don't think about that. Think about having fun instead!

She was right. I had a tendency towards the maudlin. 'A sour child,' was how I'd heard my mother describe me once, the intimation clear: I was a curse rather than a blessing.

Glancing again out of the window, at the world in white, I had to say the idea of having fun did appeal. I didn't mean to be sour, I honestly didn't.

"Come on, then," I said, crossing over to my chest of drawers and pulling out some warm clothing. "But we have to be quiet, promise me you'll be quiet."

I'm always quiet!

That was a lie. As I've said before she could interact with the material world on occasion, although I know it took it out of her. When she did I wouldn't see her for ages, sometimes up to a week – she had to rest, that's what she'd tell me when she eventually resurfaced. But on that occasion when Mum was hitting me, she'd interacted then; she threw Mum's favourite vase against the far wall, smashing it to pieces. That had stopped Mum in her tracks. More than that, it had caused her to flee from the room. Ultimately, it also caused her to hate me more.

She doesn't hate you.

"She does," I murmured back. But in that moment I didn't care, not when there was fun to be had.

Together we left my room. The landing was in darkness, no sound at all in the house except the low hum of snoring from my parents' room. Everyone was fast asleep.

God, I was excited. Such a rare but welcome feeling and all because of the snow. It has such magic to it, being both soft and pretty. I dream of it snowing in wintertime, of the outside looking just like a Christmas card. Living in the south it's rare, but tonight it was here and I didn't want to wait until morning to go out in it. In the morning, it might be gone.

I giggled. My twin swung around, almost as startled by the sound as I was.

Shush.

"Sorry," I whispered, but in truth I wasn't sorry at all. I *wanted* to giggle.

There's a creak at the top of everyone's staircase, isn't there? Certainly there was at the top of mine, but I knew where it was and how to avoid it. On the first tread, I clamped my hand around the bannister and used it to guide me, although my eyes had adjusted quickly enough to the darkness – they always did.

At the bottom we stopped and looked around us. There was still silence.

Go on then.

I crossed over to the door, placed my hand on the latch and pulled. As soon as the door opened a blast of icy air enveloped me, sharp and invigorating. As for the snow, it was falling in earnest, transforming what was once an ordinary street on the outskirts of town into a winter wonderland. With no one to disturb it, the snow was immaculate, sparkling – not just on the ground, but the air glittered too. I wanted to fall to my knees and breathe it in; taste how pure it was. But my legs moved backwards instead of forwards.

My twin was horrified.

What are you doing?

"I can't."

Why?

"Mum."

She's asleep!

She was, but she was a restless sleeper. So was I, and because of that I'd catch her coming into my room at night to stare down at me, my eyes screwed shut in pretence of sleep, but knowing the disgust and disappointment that would be on her face.

"I have to go back."

Straightaway, my twin started to plead.

She won't know. I promise. Come out, just for a few minutes.

"She *always* knows."

In some ways Mum was as intuitive as me.

Ness, come on.

Ignoring her, I closed the door on such an incredible sight, and with my heart breaking just a little bit I turned around and retraced my footsteps.

Ness!

Go away.

Often I spoke out loud to her, but not on this occasion, not here on the stairs.

If you don't stop, I'll… I'll throw something, and cause a commotion.

I stopped and glared at her. *Don't you dare! Don't you bloody dare!*

I hate swearing, even now as an adult I abhor it, but I swore then. My twin recoiled. She knew I meant it, knew I'd freeze her out if she continued to threaten me. I'd ignore her and could keep it up for days, weeks even. She hated that, more than anything.

Sulkily, she followed me to my bedroom, where I closed the curtains, tore off my clothes and returned to bed, any thought of midnight capers – of fun – banished.

You're a spoilsport.

"Shut up."

Just five minutes, that's all I was asking.

"I have to sleep."

But the snow…

"So what about the snow! Why should it even matter to you? You can't feel it on your skin; you can't taste it on your tongue or build anything with your hands. You're dead!"

There was a pause, and then a heavy sigh as I pulled the sheets over my head.

Do you know something, Ness?

"What?" I mumbled from beneath the covers, just as sulky as her.

Sometimes I think I'm more alive than you are.

Chapter One

1987

MINCH Point Lighthouse on Skye's most westerly tip –
what a place to find yourself during a month as fierce as
November. It's such a beautiful island, so dramatic, with
the scenery far exceeding my expectations. When it can be
seen, that is.

Right now, the rapidly fading light as well as the lowering clouds have conspired to obscure the mountains to one
side and the sea that rages in front. Even the sky looks as if
it's been swallowed up. All I can hear is the slashing rain
and the birds that live at the cliff's edge shrieking in protest
– thousands of them, getting as battered as I was.

"We'd better hurry," my companion shouted, a man a
couple of years younger than me, twenty-three to my twenty-five, and a typical rugged Scot: tall – well over six foot,
with wild hair that he constantly pushed out of his eyes.

Rather than answer him, I lowered my head and pushed
forwards, having to battle with the elements every step of
the way. Who knew that rain could be such a harsh foe? In
the south it's never as bad. This is *hard* rain, merciless.
How do the natives stand it?

The first structure – some kind of cabin – stood apart
from the main building, Angus having parked his car as

close to it as he could. It might have only been a few yards, but I doubted whether I could actually reach it. This rain was going to drive me to my knees.

"Ouch! Shit!"

I tripped over a boulder – the ground being littered with them. I wore boots, jeans, and a black quilted coat, all of which got soaked. As for my jeans, one knee ripped.

Immediately Angus offered his hand. "Here, Ness. I'll pull you up."

Within seconds I was on my feet again and I glanced down at my injured knee, noticed a red smear – blood. But I had no time to deal with it; we needed to get this over with.

The cabin walls looked solid enough but the windows were smashed and the door had long since blown away, smashed to pieces perhaps on the rocks below. Even so, it offered a semblance of respite, one that I was grateful for.

"Away in with you, Ness, we can wait here for a while, catch our breath."

"A while?" I'd wait here all night if needs be. This wasn't just 'fine Scottish weather' as Angus's mother had insisted when we left her house nearly an hour ago to come here, 'a wee bit of a drizzle' – this was a full-on storm!

Standing just inside the cabin, shaking the water from my hair and clapping my hands frantically together in a bid to warm up, I tried but failed to stop myself from snapping at him. "Why couldn't this have waited 'til morning?"

His reddish hair plastered to his face, as my dark hair was plastered to mine, he looked part sheepish, part deter-mined. "It's not the same in daylight, it's at night this place comes alive." Sheepish started to dominate. "Sorry, that's a bit of a conundrum, isn't it?"

Not sure how to answer that, I dug my torch out of my coat pocket instead and shone it along a short corridor that ran to the right of me.

"Oh Christ, look! There's still furniture in here. A fridge it looks like, with some sort of mould all over it, a table and chairs too." Changing direction, I shone the light directly in front of me. It was another room, smaller, with a toilet and sink in it, a *filthy* toilet and sink. Sludge or slurry covered the floor. I wrinkled my nose and had to look away. "Charming."

"Aye, that it's not," Angus agreed, or at least I think he was agreeing.

Curiosity got the better of me and I made my way down the corridor. A few steps later, I was standing in the main room. It was compact in size, the fridge not covered in mould as I first thought, but rust. A microwave, perched on top of it, had suffered a similar fate and in one corner there were bunk beds, duvets and pillows still present, although forming a crumpled, festering heap. The floor was littered with rubbish, which included old carrier bags, blankets that were in as bad a state as the duvet and pillows; bottles that had once contained alcohol or water; food wrappers and cigarette butts. On a round table lay a single plastic spatula, and facing the bunk bed were three cheap Formica units, with a sink and a hob set in. I wondered if water still flowed from the taps and crossed over to see. The cold was difficult to turn. Angus saw what I was doing and decided to help.

"Here you go," he said, "it still works."

There was a bang in the pipes somewhere, after which a sludgy mixture poured forth. I eyed it in the beam of my torch. "After a fashion," I replied. When he'd turned the tap off, I shone my torch at him, aiming low so as not to blind him. "What is this building?"

There was both excitement and fear in his eyes; a look I've seen often enough, especially when people first find out about me, when they realise what I am: a psychic, someone who can sense – who can see – the dead. Such a discovery tends to ignite both emotions, *twin* emotions.

"This is the cabin, or the bunkhouse if you like. It's where a young lad, or a couple of lads, assisting the light-house keeper would live. It's that bit removed from the main structure."

"It's more private?"

"Aye, for all parties concerned."

Inadvertently, I kicked a bottle lying in front of me. "But that was a long time ago, wasn't it? Since then I gath-er it's just been used for parties."

Angus shrugged. In the half-light he looked so much younger than his twenty-three years, a stark contrast to me who always feels double my age, weighed down by this supposed 'gift' that most of the time hangs like a weight around my neck. "There's not many come to party here, to be honest." He paused. "Not after what happened."

A ghost – that's what happened – or rather something supernatural. The very thing that lured bored teenagers to the lighthouse in the first place: the rumour that it was haunted. A building abandoned in the seventies – *suddenly* abandoned – by all those who lived on site: the lighthouse keeper, his family and whoever worked for him at the time – a lad or lads, as Angus had inferred. And it was never lived in again. It was just… abandoned. All tools downed and belongings left behind, with no reason for the sudden

11

flight ever found.

I was here because the property was for sale and a hotel-ier was interested in buying it, but not until it had been 'cleansed' – especially of its recent reputation. As well as being a native of Skye, Angus was the nephew of this Lon-don-based hotelier, who'd got in touch with me because of a case I'd been working on in my hometown of Sussex, assisting the police who were investigating the murder of two children. The information I'd provided, after contact-ing one of the victims psychically, led to the unearthing of their bodies in a lonely woodland spot. A grisly case, it continued to haunt me – the sound of the child crying, her loneliness, her sheer terror and bewilderment, how pitiful she'd been – but then so much haunted me, the child's cry was just one of many. Because of my success with that case my name had been leaked to the local press; something the constable in charge promised wouldn't happen. I worked so hard to play my involvement down, to *deny* the extent of it, to try and prevent it from ever reaching the attention of my remaining family. It had, however, reached the at-tention of some people, the hotelier for one – who'd finally persuaded me, via Angus, to investigate. Vast sums of money had been offered, but I'd only accepted enough to cover travel expenses, with lodging expenses being non-existent as Angus's mother was hosting me. The case of Minch Point Lighthouse, and what had happened here, as well as the Isle of Skye itself – more remote than anywhere I'd ever been – intrigued me. And if I could help the living as well as the dead… well, it made my 'gift' easier to bear.

A crash from outside made me jump.

"Is that thunder?" I asked.

"Probably."

I was incredulous. "So now there's going to be thunder and lightning?"

"You're not frightened of a bit of lightning are you?"

"Well, no… not unless I get struck by it."

"Does that tend to happen often with witches?"

At once my hackles rose. "What did you say?"

He coloured. Even in the dim light I could see that – his cheeks flaming as red as his hair. "I'm sorry, I didn't mean to—"

"I'm not a witch and neither am I a performing monkey. If you ever refer to me as such again, I'm leaving. You can solve the mystery of this lighthouse yourself."

"But my uncle—"

"And you can explain to him why too."

"I'm sorry, I really am."

I wasn't about to backtrack just because he'd issued an apology. "You should be."

"About what happened here—"

"Tell me."

"It didn't actually happen here, in this cabin I mean, it happened in the main building."

"We'll explore the main building soon enough."

"You're a tough wee thing, aren't you?" he said.

"And that worries you, does it?"

He looked amused, or it could have been bemused. "Actually, I'm impressed."

"And don't get any romantic notions either of wooing this 'tough wee thing'. I'm here on a job, that's all."

He almost spluttered when I said that. "Perish the thought," was his eventual response as he turned from me and walked over to the window to stare outwards at the sea.

"I'll make no secret of it," he started to say, just as a bolt of lightning lit up the sky. "I used to come here plenty as a youngster too. Ach, can you blame me? Can you blame any of us? You're short on entertainment when you live in a place like this, believe me. And the lighthouse, well, it's remote; it's got shelter, plenty of dark corners if you fancy a smooch with one of the lasses. You can get up to what you like because the adults tend to stay away." Facing me again, he carried on. "Obviously there's drink involved, beer, cider, whatever the kids can get hold of. In my day it was cider, but the hard stuff creeps in now, as you can see by the bottles at your feet: gin, vodka, whisky, and occasionally drugs."

I raised an eyebrow at this but let him carry on.

"For years there's a game we've played at the lighthouse called Thirteen Ghost Stories. Have you heard of it?"

I shook my head, whilst he glanced fretfully over in the direction of the main complex. Another roll of thunder made him flinch this time, not me.

"It's a sort of ritual, I suppose. A bunch of us gather together and light thirteen candles – you know, those wee tea light things."

"Yes, I know," I responded.

"You sit in a circle, and each of you takes turns in telling a story."

"A short story I presume, as there's thirteen to get through?"

"Aye, mostly it's just a few paragraphs, although Maire MacTavish used to go on a bit. She's an author now by the way, written a romance book. Have you heard of her?"

"I don't tend to read romance." At least not anymore.

"You don't? Now there's a surprise. Anyway, as each

ghost story is told, you blow out a candle, counting all the way to thirteen. You can imagine it, can't you, the room getting darker and darker, the shadows around you becoming more menacing."

I could, the stories getting wilder too, macabre even.

"The best story is always saved 'til last. In my time it was Gordy Ballantyne who usually bagged that honour, he had a brutal mind, so he did. The stuff he'd make up, whoa, even now I try not to think of it. He was into blood and guts, was Gordy. Once he'd terrified the shit out of us – oops, sorry, excuse my language: the living bejezus; he'd blow the last candle out. By this stage, the darkness," Angus paused, took a breath, "…was intense."

"What would happen then?" I realised I was holding my breath too; there was even a break in the weather – a lull – as if the rain, the wind, and the sea itself was curious.

"Angus?"

"Nothing!" he declared. "Absolutely bloody nothing. We'd all fall about laughing, some would start chasing each other around the room, shouting 'woo woo' at the tops of our voices, tickling each other, laughing, joking, and a fair bit of flirting too. And that was it, honestly – there was no drama, not really. For years that game's been played here. And it was fun, just a wee bit of fun." He lowered his head, solemn all of a sudden. "Until now that is. This new generation, they might be wilder in some ways, but basically they're good kids. And Ally Dunn, she's not a liar or a drama queen. I've known her all her life. She's changed, all those involved that night have changed." Once more he stared out of the cracked window. "I'm wondering if they'll ever be the same again."

Chapter Two

1972

COME on, play the game; I want to play it.

"Mum's only in the kitchen."

So, switch to thought instead.

I did as she asked. *What's the point though?*

The point is that we all need a name.

I don't know your name.

Ask her.

Ask Mum? I don't think so!

Make one up.

I've made up hundreds for you in the past; you don't like any of them.

That's because... because...

None of them are your real name.

I'd hit the nail on the head.

It's not fair! It's so not fair!

Oh, please don't start.

It's not though, is it? I didn't ask to be born dead.

I winced; it always came back to this. *I'm sorry I lived.*

And I meant it, I honestly did. Perhaps I would have felt differently if I were 'normal', like my brothers and my sisters who all got on well enough with my mother. But I wasn't. And yes, that made me sorry at times that I continued to breathe.

It's all right, Ness, don't get sad.

As guilty as she made me feel, as frustrated, even as scared at times, she cared this twin of mine and she wanted me to care for her too. I was born ten years ago and I was supposed to have a sister – an *identical* sister. When my mother realised what had happened to one of us, she'd screamed apparently, wouldn't stop screaming. It had been a difficult pregnancy – I remember Mum referring several times to how ill she'd been whilst carrying us. It'd been a difficult birth too. Not to have a full return on it must have been a harsh blow. One of my brothers, Ollie, had once elaborated further on this tale of misery, had seemed to take great delight in telling me. It wasn't just grief that did for her apparently, she'd haemorrhaged too, losing blood and becoming weaker. The doctors whisked both babies away, but what they did with the deceased I don't know. Afterwards, Mum was ill for days, weeks even. The whole experience had changed her entirely.

Very early on I realised she could hardly stand to look at me; certainly I can't remember ever being hugged or kissed by her. I have a theory about this: instead of appreciating what she'd got, Mum dwelt only on what she'd lost. I was always such a painful reminder. Then, as time wore on, it became clearer what else I was. A young child doesn't know how to lie, to pretend that what's happening isn't – and the gulf between us widened.

My twin was talking again.

I like the name Mary.

Mary?

Does it suit me?

No, you're not angelic enough.

She laughed at that.

Lorraine?

I screwed up my nose. *I don't like Lorraine.*

So what? It's my name, not yours.

You haven't got a name.

Yet, she reminded me. *Okay, okay, Sandra. Maybe.*

No, I've gone off that already. Carrie?

Carrie's good.

Shall I be Carrie?

If you want to, it's up to you.

Ness, you need to take this seriously.

Carrie's fine.

You're not taking it seriously!

I am. I like Carrie. We haven't had that one before.

But would Mum have chosen it?

Mum? I've told you, I don't know.

What name would Mum have chosen, do you think?

She can be relentless at times.

Getting up to turn the volume on the TV louder, she knew what I was doing: trying to drown her out. From being a vague outline, she materialised more fully to stand in front of me. Like looking in a mirror; she had the same straight black hair, a heart-shaped face, pale skin, and dark eyes. Only one thing was different – her stormy expression.

Ask Mum!

I can't.

I want you to ask her.

It'll only upset her. Or make her angry, one of the two.

Ask her or I'll scratch you!

You can't hurt me and you know it.

I can! I will!

She never used to get so angry, upset yes, but not angry, not whilst we were growing up. It sounds odd saying that my twin was growing up too, but she was, in the spirit world at least. It wasn't that I didn't care about how frustrated she felt at times; I did, especially with regards to my mother. She seemed to *crave* her attention. My father, brothers and sisters, she didn't seem so bothered about, but then neither was I to an extent.

Ask her, Ness.

Or what?

Or… or… I'll make the TV go blurry.

Big deal.

I didn't like giving in to her too often, if I did, it encouraged her and she'd be worse the next time. I turned from her, from the TV, and settled back into the sofa, carrying on with the book I was reading as part of my homework – a somewhat dull book, written for kids, but not able to capture a kid's imagination; a shame because I loved reading usually.

Hanging around for a few minutes, huffing and puffing, she then disappeared. *Good*, I thought, *she's left me in peace* – for a short while at least.

I should have known better.

She appeared again, dashing the book from my hands. That's what she'd been doing during her brief absence, gathering enough energy to do that.

I jumped up; glad that I was alone in the room, that no one else had seen it.

Why'd you do that?

You're mean.

I'm not.

You are.

19

Because I won't ask Mum? Of course I won't. You know what she'll do.

But I need to know.

No!

Ask her or I'll hurt you, I will. I can do it. I'm strong enough.

Her insistence – her *threats* – incensed me further. I wouldn't do what she asked, never! Besides which, who could hurt me more, her or Mum? Mum wasn't averse to beating me, and sometimes those beatings were severe – as if she was trying to beat my 'ability' right out of me, perhaps in her own way, trying to save me. That's how she always justified it. Not that she ever said as much out loud. But sometimes I could catch what she was thinking – *I'm doing this for her own good, something's not right with her, something's very wrong, I have to do this, it's for her own benefit* – and all the while Dad would stand by, not joining in, but not stopping her either. Only once did he do that, after my Aunt Jean's funeral when I'd seen her spirit at the wake, when I'd said I'd seen her, when I'd made that mistake. Dad had to pull Mum off me then, fearing that she'd go too far, that she'd send me to join my twin. Every other time he endured, as I endured.

I stormed past my twin, warning her not to follow.

I WANT TO KNOW MY NAME!

When I didn't reply, she screamed again.

FIND OUT MY NAME!

I swung round, as enraged as her.

"You haven't got a name! I expect Mum didn't bother to give you one and if she did, she never told me, no one has. I don't even know where you're buried, *if* you're buried that is. You might not be. You're just… nothing. Do you hear me? You *should* be nothing!"

I realised my mistake too late.

"Not this again."

Drawn by my shouting, my mother had entered the living room. As I swung round, she was there in front of me, her face a mask of barely controlled fury, and I cowered in her shadow. Why had I done it? Why had I started screaming? What had possessed me?

You, you possessed me!

I glowered at my twin; she'd hurt me after all, by proxy.

Mum's hand came out to grab me by the scruff of my neck, I knew that any moment that same hand would hurl me across the room and I'd go smashing into the wall. And then she'd grab me again, by my hair or the collar of my blouse and she'd stand me up in front of her, freeing one hand so that she could slap my face, not once but several times.

I started whimpering. "It's because she wants to know her name, she *needs* to know."

No matter what Mum did to me, nothing could hurt as much as her words.

"A mistake, that's what she was, as were you. You should have both died that day."

Chapter Three

THERE are some games that shouldn't be played, the most obvious perhaps being the Ouija. The reason for that is because there's a belief system involved – and belief has a habit of opening doorways, ones that should remain firmly shut. This game that Angus was telling me about – Thirteen Ghost Stories – sounded more like a ritual. He'd even called it that himself, carried out in this same place, in the same manner, time after time, year after year, mostly by kids, the young, the innocent, the *enthusiastic*, their hearts and minds willing something to happen, throwing caution aside for the sake of a thrill, praying even. *Come on, come on, whatever's out there, break through the veil that separates us, we're desperate to see you.* The energy, the thoughts, the hopes, and the dreams build up, until finally something in the darkness *does* takes notice. They stop, they listen to your pleas, and they step forward, eager to see you too. Not always for the best of reasons.

The man who stood in front of me mentioned that all those involved that night had changed, but he'd changed too. Just minutes beforehand, he'd been gung-ho about bringing me here and showing me around, intrigued to see what I could sense. But now, with his eyes on the main building, reticence had set in.

"How long is it since you've been to the lighthouse, Angus?"

He rubbed at his chin. "It's the kids that come," he repeated. "Not the adults."

"So a few years then?"

He nodded.

"And what happened to Ally Dunn, it was two months ago?"

"Aye."

"Any chance of seeing her at some point?"

"We can ask her mother."

There was something else I needed to know, something that risked unsettling him further. "Angus, has there been a known death at the lighthouse?" According to the research I'd been able to do prior to my visit, there hadn't been, the hotelier and Angus's mother confirming that, but I hadn't asked Angus outright yet, and I'd deliberately used the word 'known'. Not everything catches the eye of the media, especially on an island like this: remote and with a strong sense of community. Some things get hushed up.

He didn't answer straight away, in fact, he didn't answer at all. Another almighty roar captured our attention, the wind so loud it hurt your ears.

"We should get going," Angus yelled.

"To the main building?"

"Aye."

The lighthouse complex proper, not this single cabin that, although abandoned too, seemed benign enough. Perhaps 'benign' wasn't quite the right word, for, while I could feel nothing of a tangible nature, it certainly had a simmering quality – a precursor perhaps to what lay ahead. As we left the building my eyes were drawn back to the fridge, the microwave, which were covered in rust. I shone my torch at them again. *Diseased*, that's what they looked like, as did this building, and the buildings that surrounded it.

That thought having formed in my head I couldn't wait to leave, to take my chances with the great outdoors again, with what was natural rather than otherwise. That's the thing, you see, there are those that think because I'm psychic I welcome what I see, that I take it in my stride, and it's simply part of who I am. That's not the case though. To date, I've not met a single person with abilities similar to mine who actively welcomes it. If anything, I've seen madness in their eyes, and desperation. I've recognised that in myself too.

The cold rain was at once enlivening and repellent, and we'd get soaked again dashing from here to there, but what did it matter? I only hoped that when we got back Angus's mother had plenty of hot water, so I could take a shower and warm my bones. There'd been grass beneath my feet en route to the cabin but now there was gravel, no crunch could be heard as such. It was the change in texture that was obvious. I tried to look up, to get an impression of the building before me, licking my lips as I did and noticing the salt on them. It seemed sizeable enough, laid out over two floors rather than one. The door was intact and Angus shoved against it with his shoulder three or four times. When it opened – quite suddenly – he stumbled, falling across the threshold. On his feet again, he shut the door behind me, having to fight to do that too as I shone the torch around. A smell was the first thing to assail me, one that made my eyes water. It was a mixture of things, damp, rot and mould, but there was an underlying sweetness to it, one that was sickly rather than pleasant. Swallowing hard, I continued to peer into the gloom.

What a mess – an *unholy* mess you could say. There was a sofa and two armchairs, both of them vomiting stuffing. A low coffee table had been turned over and rag-like curtains hung at the windows. On the floor, torn pages were scattered everywhere.

"They're from school exercise books," Angus informed me when I remarked upon them. "I suppose you could call it another ritual. Students come here at the end of their school year and they tear their books to pieces. It's a sort of celebration if you like, a release."

I supposed it was.

As in the cabin, there were empty bottles too, scores of them, and the wallpaper looked as if giant fingernails had travelled up and down it, scoring it again and again. Directing my torch upwards, I noticed that the ceiling had cracks in it, reminding me of a spider's web.

As I'd had to do in the cabin, I kicked a path clear in front of me. "How many rooms are there in this building altogether?"

"There's this room, which is the living room."

"Obviously."

"A kitchen of course, a utility room, three bedrooms and a bathroom."

"How many children did the keeper have?"

"Two. A boy and a girl."

"Is this where you played the game, in the living room?"

He shook his head. "No, we used to play it upstairs in the bedroom."

"Whose bedroom?"

"Not the main bedroom, it was one of the kids'."

"Any reason why?"

He shrugged. "The main bedroom belonged to the mum and dad, it seemed a bit… pervy, to go in there, where they, erm…" A burst of laughter escaped him. "Teens, eh? It's funny the way we used to think."

I couldn't help but smile too. "Tell me about the family."

"I never knew them, but according to everyone round here they were a strange lot, insular, you know? Och, don't get me wrong, island folk can be like that, non-island folk too. There's plenty who away up to Skye to escape, those who want to keep themselves to themselves, but as keepers of the lighthouse, you'd think they'd mingle. They're a vital part of the community with an important role to play. Caitir and Niall were the kids' names, the girl was the elder of the two, but they never went to school, they were taught at home. The family lived here for around five years, until 1977. They'd come from Barra—"

"Barra?" I interrupted. "Where's that?"

"It's a Hebridean island, a real outpost, but where they went to, no one knows. It was a cold day in winter when they ceased whatever they were doing and left, they didn't even bother to turn the TV off. It was still on full blast when it was discovered what had happened." Clearly he disapproved. "It's against the rules you know, to do that, for a light keeper to just leave. Someone needs to remain on site at all times to ensure the light comes on when it's supposed to. Later, one of my dad's friends checked with The Northern Lighthouse Board whether the Camerons had been reassigned elsewhere."

"And?"

"They hadn't."

"Little wonder. What about the boys that helped Mr Cameron? Did they leave too?"

"It was just the one boy by that time, a young lad called Liam, and he'd been dismissed a few months earlier. Mr Cameron said he had no need of him, that it was a waste of money employing him, that he and his wife could manage well enough."

"Is Liam still on the island?"

"No, he left at the first opportunity, a lot of the youngsters do, to be fair. They go to Glasgow or Edinburgh. Unless you're into farming, there's not much to stick around for."

"Has Liam still got family on Skye?"

"Aye, his dad's here, Ron McCarron."

"Perhaps I can talk to him."

Angus snorted. "Good luck in finding him sober enough to make sense."

"Oh," I responded.

"Oh indeed."

"When was the lighthouse put on the market?"

"Only recently, a whole ten years later. In this part of the world, things have a tendency to move slowly, business included. As you know, my uncle really wants to invest in it. He said it'd make a mint as a bespoke guesthouse, that the punters would love its quirkiness. There are those on Skye that doubt that, who think it's in too remote a location to stay busy all year-round, but Uncle Glenn insists that's not a problem, that people will flock here, come rain, shine, hail or snow. And they may do if what happened to Ally gets fixed."

I nodded, mulling over in my mind what he'd said and what I knew already. Ally Dunn had barely spoken a word in the two months since she'd been here. She and a group of her friends had sat upstairs, as so many had done on so many occasions before, and played Thirteen Ghost Stories. There'd actually been thirteen of them that night according to Angus, usually there were a lot fewer, each of them telling a story, and, as they'd counted upwards, got closer to thirteen, things started to happen. Several of the teenagers experienced blinding headaches, another two felt sick, one to the point of retching. One girl swore blind that the teenager next to her had pinched her, whilst a boy felt someone blowing into his face, a short sharp puff that caused his eyes to water profusely. But, of course, it was Ally who'd suffered the most.

"Poor Ally," Angus was saying, looking around him, at the shadows that seemed to be on the increase. His hands were in front of him, the fingernails of one hand scratching the palm of the other – a nervous habit perhaps? If so, I didn't blame him. Just as he was nervous, I was too. I wasn't sure what was here, yet – but there *was* something. And its energy... was it dark or was it troubled? There's a difference as far as I'm concerned. Troubled I could identify with more, whereas the dark verges on something I don't want to believe exists – worse than any human savagery, it's something inhuman.

I took a breath, reminding myself what I was here to do: to discover if this place was haunted or if what happened to Ally Dunn was the result of teenage imagination, which is fertile enough at the best of times, never mind the worst. "I need to know everything you know."

"Well, it was... erm... Christ, it's hard to get the words out, you know, standing here..."

"But here is where it happened?"

"Like I said, it was upstairs, in the one of the kid's rooms."

"Which kid?"

"The girl's."

He meant Caitir's room – a private room, a sanctuary, or at least it should have been.

I glanced upwards at the ceiling, at the cracks similar to a spider's web and made a decision. "Then we'll do the same, Angus, we'll go upstairs. You can tell me there."

Chapter Four

1973

NESS, Ness, don't cry. Mum really doesn't hate you.
  She does!
  She doesn't, she just gets… angry sometimes. So do you.
  Me?

I was upstairs again, in my room, the only place I could find respite from the rest of my family, where they didn't usually bother me. Only my twin *bothered* me. There'd been yet another argument between Mum and me, or rather Mum had laid into me for yet another perceived slight. I'd been lying on my bed sobbing, but at my twin's words I sat bolt upright. "This has got nothing to do with me. This is her fault, hers and… and yours."

Her pale eyes clouded, as her shoulders wilted. *Feeble*, I thought, *that's what she looks like*, and then immediately felt guilty. Another thing that had been pointed out to me several times by my mother was that I'd been the twin who took all the nutrients from the other one. 'Greedy,' she'd called me once. I'd had to bite down hard on my tongue so I wouldn't retaliate. How the hell could anyone blame a foetus! But I had been greedy, even if unwittingly, stealing my sister's life force to bolster my own. Staring at her, I started to reach out, to touch her arm, an apology forming on my lips, but I stopped, and couldn't go through with it. Instead, I snatched my arm back and threw more words at her.

"I wish you'd all leave me alone."

Ness—

"Mum, Dad, my dumb brothers and sisters, but most of all I mean you. How can I ever hope to be normal when you're always hanging around?"

The way she sat there, huddled on the edge of my bed, only served to infuriate me more. She was doing it deliberately, I was sure of it, acting all pathetic in order to try and make me sorry for her, to admit how horrid I was being. It wasn't going to work, not this time. I shoved my face into hers, expecting her to recoil, and was surprised when she didn't.

"I hate you, do you know that?"

Ness, don't.

"I don't want to live with ghosts."

But it's your gift.

I laughed, such a bitter sound. "Being able to see you, to see others, is *not* a gift!"

It is, Ness.

She always said this, always!

"If I could unsee you, I would."

You can't unsee things. That isn't even a proper word.

"How do you know? How the heck do you know? You don't go to school."

I'm not stupid; I know a lot of things, as much as you do, if not more.

"Then keep it to yourself and don't bother me with it."

She was the one who tried to reach out, but I reared back.

"Don't touch me," I spat.

In truth, what always surprised me whenever she did touch me was the warmth of her. She wasn't cold at all, not like I expected her to be, she was as warm as anything living.

You don't always hate seeing me.

"I do," I replied, wiping at the tears that threatened to spill.

Sometimes we have fun.

"No we don't!"

But that wasn't strictly true. We *could* have had fun together, plenty of it – like that time last year when the snow came, we could have gone out together, played and laughed. God knows I had very few friends as well as a family who either treated me as an outcast or a joke. Yes, there had been some who'd tried to befriend such a solemn child, but when you think your own family doesn't like you, you simply can't believe that strangers will either. And so it's easier to shun people before they shun you, it's easier to be alone. Especially when you *weren't* alone. When you could see others hovering around the little girl that's smiling at you or the boy who's asked you to join in a game of tag – attachments, spirits, some inviting you, or rather pleading with you to help them, to acknowledge them, to admit you can see them. The despair on their faces as you shake your head, as you walk away, their terror that someone might never see them again, that wasn't fun, none of it. It was too much for someone who was just a little girl as well.

Ness.

She was tugging at me now.

Ness, everything will be all right, if you'd just accept me.

Anger caused my chest to heave.

I'm the only family you really need.

My breath was coming in short, sharp pants.

The only friend.

Was she being serious?

We're a part of each other, Ness.

Still she was tugging at my sleeve, desperate for me to answer.

Finally, I raised my head and looked her straight in the eyes again.

"I hate you."

She was even more pitiful than before.

Don't keep saying that.

"Why not? Tell me a good reason why I shouldn't?"

Why? Because you're beginning to sound just like Mum, that's why.

Chapter Five

THE hallway was also littered, ankle-deep in places, and that terrible smell… it really was sickening, a real stench. We needed more light, the torch was useless against such inky blackness, but it was also the only thing we had. Ironic really, that more light was needed at the lighthouse. It defied its existence alone on the cliff top and it defied its name too.

"Why was this lighthouse decommissioned?" I asked, as we found the stairwell and began to climb, Angus insisting on going ahead of me. "Was another one built?"

"Aye," he couldn't keep the shiver out of his voice, "there's one further up the coast, just a tower, no big house or cabins attached to it and therefore much more cost effective. After the Camerons left, this lighthouse was converted to automatic operation for a while, but the light kept failing, and for no reason that they could fathom, so it was decided to build another. That one works well enough. Mind you, with satellite marine navigation coming on in leaps and bounds, by my reckoning, in ten to twenty years, there'll be no need for lighthouses at all. There'll be loads of them up and down the country, left like this, abandoned, the new tower a few miles away included, the lights turned off forevermore."

It was a sobering thought.

At the top of the stairs, on the landing, we stood side by side. More darkness stretched before us, and in that darkness were deeper patches – doorways to bedrooms, which at this moment felt like they harboured other dimensions, ones we weren't equipped for.

Striving to keep my breathing calm, to keep it even, I nonetheless had to reach into the pocket of the coat I was wearing. In it I'd placed a great big chuck of obsidian, my hand closing around it and feeling how solid it was, how cool, its black shiny surface as smooth as glass. A lucky charm, a talisman, call it what you will, it gave me comfort. Renowned for its ability to repel negativity, to protect a person from psychic attack, it was also supposed to have healing qualities, helping to release lower or negative emotions – I hadn't found it much good for that, but it was certainly a stone I was drawn to at the moment, more than tourmaline, which was widely considered the queen of the protection stones. It was *my* stone and without it I felt exposed. Having drawn strength from the crystal, I inhaled again and composed myself as much as possible, given the circumstances. That feeling that there was something here – besides Angus and myself – was becoming more apparent. There *was* something and it was watching – hiding in shadows that were darker still.

"Come on," Angus said, either getting braver or wanting to get this whole shebang over and done with as quickly as possible. "The girl's room is this way."

My conflict continued. Should we be doing this – going into what might be the epicentre? Maybe it was best if I went alone, I didn't want anything to happen to Angus. Another option: we could call the whole thing off and seek more advice. It's not as if I fancied putting myself in danger either. But here we were – just feet from Caitir's room. It might be possible to make contact, and if we did, we could wrap this whole matter up tonight and what few days I'd booked here I could enjoy instead, taking long solitary walks beside lochs and along cliff tops, immersing myself in the beauty of Skye, which might prove healing too. Hope – how it spurs a person on. And despite my fear I *was* hopeful. I also reminded myself of other encounters I'd had previously; spirits that seemed as dark as this one, as spiteful, and as mischievous. They'd all been human once, humans who had suffered, and in the spirit realm were suffering still. That was what kept them grounded. So often – as with the girls in the woods, certainly the one I'd managed to contact anyway – it was shock, hurt, despair and disbelief at what had happened to them, that people, living and breathing, could inflict such cruelty, could be so merciless. What if, like her, something terrible had happened to whoever was grounded here: what if it was experiencing a similar range of emotions and having lost faith in this world, had lost faith in the next too? If so, that might be why it had hit out – at Ally Dunn, at the other teenagers. It had simply had enough of being teased, even if that teasing was more attributable to youthful ignorance than malice. If I could release its spirit, not leave it lingering in such a lonely, desolate spot, anger and fear growing ever more potent, then I had to try.

That little girl in the woods – she was never far from my mind, or her expression as her body was eventually found, as she'd hovered above it, staring down into milky eyes that had once shone with vitality, at a perfect complexion now mottled and dirt-encrusted. The girl was sad, of course she was, but she'd been relieved too. Finally there was resolve and because of it she could let go, her sadness fading entirely as the light wrapped itself around her. The second girl in the woods, her friend, I'd tried so hard with her too – but you have to be ready for release, you can't force it. As free-will exists in life, it seems to exist in death too. We may have found her body, lying right beside the first, but her spirit continued to elude me – she was there all right, she was grounded, but she refused to come forward. But I've made a promise: one day I'll go back to those woods, as lonely a place as this, and I'll go alone, with no police officers in tow, and try again to coax her.

Having bypassed the two other bedrooms, the bathroom as well, Angus pushed the door to the third bedroom open. I don't know what I expected; perhaps a rush of energy as whatever was grounded hurled itself at me, a mad keening perhaps from something barely visible, a burst of emotion that would force its way down my throat to broil in the pit of my stomach. My imagination runs riot as much as the next person. But there were no spectral hands to tear at my hair, no hollow eyes that bored into mine, there was nothing – absolutely nothing. It was just a dark space, into which we stared blindly – Caitir's room, only a very little of her energy lingering: the innocence, the sweetness, and the fear.

Who'd she been afraid of?

Who or what?

Outside the wind had picked up. I pictured it curling itself around the building, tendrils desperately seeking portals they could rush into, entering at last, in belligerent triumph. I envisioned the mist too as it crept stealthily inland, intent on suffocating us.

I gulped. "Angus, I think we should come back in day—
"

It wasn't him who interrupted me; it was a high-pitched cry that rang on and on.

"It's just the weather," he said.

"I know that."

"It can sound pretty eerie at times."

That was the understatement of the year. But he was right, it *was* just the weather and I needed to keep calm. This was my profession. I couldn't run at the slightest hint of unease. I discarded entirely what I was going to say earlier. "Let's go further in."

We did, Angus at my heel.

"Shall we close the door?" he asked.

"Leave it open."

"The wind might catch it, that's all."

It might. We'd see.

"So now, tell me everything that happened," I said, steeling myself, imagining not what was lurking, or the elements as a living beast, but a swathe of pure white light, drawn straight from the beating heart of the universe, bold and brilliant. A shield, that's what the light was, one that no dark force had the power to penetrate. Immediately, I could feel my shoulders relax and my jaw unclench. I could do this. We were safe… or safe enough.

"It was a wild and stormy night," he began, "similar to this one…"

Immediately I reprimanded him. "Angus! Come on, kill the jokes."

"Sorry," he replied, laughing and then he paused again. "Actually it's not a joke. It *was* a wild and stormy night, as many of them are on Skye. The kids had gathered here

38

again, probably a couple of the older ones had borrowed their parents' cars or something and were looking forward to another night of partying. But I think they looked forward to the game the most – I know we used to, when we were young. It added that extra bit of spice. They'd drank, mucked around a bit, the usual, and then they'd settled down – this is along the lines of what I've been told, by the way, by one of the lads who was here. I can't give you a blow by blow account, it was hard enough getting this much out of him."

"Okay," I conceded, shivering a little. "It'll do for now."

"The candles were lit, thirteen of them, and then everyone took their place, sitting in a circle. The first person told their story, blew out the candle, the next, and the next, and so on. There'd be giggles, a bit of elbowing to hush the gigglers up, one teen clutching onto another, any excuse, eh? But as the stories continued, the atmosphere must have changed, that clutching became pinching, people no longer laughing. They'd started to accuse each other of stuff, getting tetchy. During all of this, Ally had grown quieter, those either side of her, Isabel and Craig, had noticed but not said a word, to her or each other. It was as if she'd gone into a trance, Craig said. She was just... staring."

Coming to a halt, it took a few seconds for him to continue.

"Finally they got to the last story, which is always a tense time. Soon the room would be in complete darkness. It was Isabel's turn to tell it, but she didn't want to, she'd got scared, the way that everyone was behaving, not sitting as quiet as they usually do, as rapt, but getting aggressive with each other. Most of all, Ally was unnerving her, her being as still as a statue. I think Isabel made some joke about not bothering with the last story, leaving the candle to burn, but the response to that was aggressive too. She was told to 'bloody get on with it.' So she did, trying to string it out a bit, to make sense of what was happening around her, but just as there's a beginning and a middle, there's an end, and so she leant forward to blow the candle out. And that's when it happened."

"What?" I asked.

"In the darkness Ally started screaming, started to tear at herself, her clothes, and her hair. She jumped up, pushing off Isabel who was trying desperately to calm her, Craig too, and almost hurling them across the room. Her strength was superhuman, Craig said, but then he had been drinking. She continued to scratch at herself, to spit and snarl, and then she stopped. Started howling instead, falling to her knees, her hands covering her face, as if trying to protect herself, all the while screaming *No! No! No!*"

My teeth began to chatter. The room was like an icebox.

"It took almost all of them to drag Ally out of this room, every single one shitting themselves by now, unsure of what she'd seen but knowing she wasn't playacting, that whatever was going on was genuine. They'd also had their own terrifying experiences to go by. As another boy said, Murdo, the air was like a firecracker, he could almost see it sizzling in front of him. They got Ally into one of the cars, three of them in the rear seats pinning her down and drove her back to her house. They were scared of what her mum and dad's reaction would be, but they'd rather take a chance with that than stay at the lighthouse. By the time they got her home she'd calmed down… and I mean seriously calmed. She was virtually catatonic. Gradually the kids dispersed, some made their own way home, others wanted their parents to come and fetch them, and Ally's mother obliged by calling them. They were shaken. They still are shaken. No one knows what happened here really, especially to Ally, and she's not saying. Ness, tell me, what can you feel?"

"Something."

"What kind of something?"

I looked around yet again; the darkness as thick as ever, the wind still moaning.

"Something that's gone back into hiding, but not for long."

Things like that never hide for long.

Chapter Six

AFTER several more minutes spent acclimatising, I reached a decision. If this thing was proving elusive, then perhaps there really was little point in hanging around further, especially as doubts had been planted in my mind as to the nature of what it actually was. I needed to find out more about the history of Minch Point – knowledge was armour too – and it'd be handy to have more light, daylight that is, to get a proper grip on where I was.

"Come on," I said. "Tomorrow I'll—"

The door that I'd asked Angus to leave open, slammed shut.

We both swung round to stare at it.

"It's the wind," Angus said finally.

"Not this time."

"How do you know?"

"I'm a psychic, remember?"

Right then the tension in that room was mounting, like a rubber band being pulled tight at both ends, and bound to snap.

"First things first," I decided. "Try the door."

It must just yield, and if it did, we'd scarper.

No such luck.

"It's stuck fast," Angus said. "I don't understand it.

There's no lock on it or anything."

"Damn," I muttered under my breath. There was nothing for it but to turn and face the darkness again. *Bright light, Ness, visualise bright light.* I had to surround both Angus and myself in it, head to toe. And stop being afraid. That was imperative. I *mustn't* show fear. "Whoever you are, whatever you're doing here, we mean no harm. We've come to help."

"We?"

I shot Angus a glance, one meant to silence him.

"My name is Ness Patterson, I'm what's called a psychic. I can see those that reside in the spirit world. If you're trapped here, if you're bewildered or you're in pain, I'll do my best to help. Communicate with me, tell me why you haven't passed, why it is that you remain."

Here's the thing: it's hard to know what to say to a grounded spirit – so often they're wary, they're terrified, they're the ones that are afraid of us. I've witnessed other supposed psychics go steamrolling in, baiting them, blaming them almost for having the temerity to remain. They make no effort whatsoever to understand the reasons why. I've seen too how the spirit reacts, how it strikes out, plays to the gallery, no matter how unwittingly. I've seen it and I don't like it. It doesn't solve a thing. And so I've developed a different technique: to go in with light, love and understanding, to realise that fear is often at the bottom of the problem – no not often – it *always* is. Fear is key.

Whatever I was addressing showed no sign of responding.

"Please talk to me. Not out loud, I don't mean that, I can hear thoughts well enough. Aren't you lonely here? There's no need to be. You're spirit now, and that's where you belong, in the spiritual world. Tell me, in the darkness, can you see a light? A bright light that is, like no light you've ever seen before, can you see it shining?"

No response, the tension still at breaking point, the wind around us as agitated as ever.

Perhaps what the entity needed was time to consider my words? That was okay, that was understandable. A two-way communication could take time.

With Angus still standing obediently beside me, I reiterated what I'd said previously.

"I really do want to help. I'm here for no other reason than that. I certainly don't want to upset you. If you let us go, I'll return – that's a promise. I won't abandon you."

Exhaling, I turned to Angus. "Perhaps the door will open now."

"I bloody hope so."

He gave it a yank, but it refused to budge. He tried several more times. "It's not moving," he complained, just as it flew open. "Oh," he exclaimed. "It's not stuck anymore."

Stuck? Surely he must have realised… Instead of contradicting him, I muttered "Good", sighing in relief that my words had had an impact. I started to make my way over to the door. We'd be out of here soon enough and I could breathe again.

Breathe?

It was only when I realised my breath was caught in my throat that the visions started – so many of them; an assault, filling my mind, one after the other. *Horrific* visions. Images I couldn't bear to see, but couldn't escape either. It's easy to shut your eyes, but your mind's eye? I hadn't learnt that trick yet. I was an easy target – a sitting duck. Whatever was in the room with us was having such fun.

God, those visions, they made me quake in my boots. Torture, people, animals – *children* – being torn apart, mutilated – innocent things, vulnerable, their eyes wide open in terror, mouths screaming.

"Stop. Stop. STOP!"

I didn't know what Angus was doing while this was happening, probably looking at me with that bemused expression of his. He couldn't see what I could see. At least I didn't think so.

"Angus," I croaked, my voice sticking in my throat, "get out. We have to get out."

"What is it, Ness? What's happened?"

So he *was* oblivious. Thank goodness.

"Have to get out," I croaked again.

"Aye, of course, the door's open now."

"Please, help."

What I want is for him to *drag* me out. I can't seem to move of my own accord.

"Angus!"

"Aye, lass, I've got you. It's okay, I'm here."

With his hand on my arm, he forced me forwards. These visions – when would they end?

Stop it! Please! Why are you doing this?

Mentally I implored, but whoever was responsible, wasn't listening. On the contrary, it was as though they *thrived* on this sort of thing – the sick and the twisted. How could they? I don't understand and I'm *glad* that I don't. But seeing is torture too.

The threshold of the doorway is too far away, every step it takes to get there nothing less than agony. *Come on, Angus! Come on.* These visions are going to kill me. Why is it always the children that suffer the most? I'm sure my

45

airways are on the verge of closing completely, that my heart will beat too fast, will buck like a wild horse. *Angus!*

I lashed out. Doesn't he know the pain I'm in? The fool!

"Hurry! I've told you to hurry!"

I want to hit him, hurt him, claw at him, and draw blood. Stupid man! Stupid, stupid, man!

"Ness, for God's sake, calm down will you." As my fist connected with his jaw he yelled out. "For Christ's sake, what's wrong with you?"

"I... I... GET ME OUT!"

His grasp on me tightening, he hurled us over the threshold, one hand releasing me temporarily so that he could close the door behind us.

"Come on." His voice is a mixture of so many things, shock, fear and anger. "You can explain what's just happened, why you attacked me, later."

Looking into his eyes, I can't see the colour of them in the darkness, but I can see how wide they are – probably as wide as my own.

Explain?

How do you explain hell?

* * *

"There now, there now, get this down you."

Angus's mother, Eilidh – pronounced *Ay-lee* I'd gathered listening to Angus referring to her previously – had tried to get me to drink a cup of tea, but I could barely hold the cup I was shaking so much. Having eyed me for a few seconds, she clearly thought something stronger was needed and handed me a tumbler of whisky instead.

"It's Talisker of course, Skye's own. My advice? Knock it

back."

I did as she suggested, the fiery liquid initially burning my throat and making my eyes water, but gradually giving way to a more pleasant smoky warmth, one I was grateful for – in the confines of Caitir's room I thought I'd never be warm again.

I could feel Angus staring. He was sitting across the table from me, in a room full of chintz: his mother's dining room. I could barely lift my eyes to meet his, but I had to.

"Angus," I began, but then stopped. His jaw looked pretty bruised and there was a scratch under his left eye. "Oh God, I'm sorry, I'm so, so sorry."

"What happened? Why'd you do it?"

His bewildered look made me feel even worse. Eilidh, I noticed, turned her gaze away, leaving it to us to sort out. I was grateful for that at least.

"Just before we left the bedroom I started to see things, terrible things."

"Like what?"

I was curious. "Did you not see anything at all?"

"Just you, going ape."

"I... well... yeah... They were visions..." I couldn't bear to recall them, but somehow I had to try. "Terrible scenes of torture and degradation. Things I could never imagine, not in a million years. They just... flooded into my mind, one after the other."

Eilidh was looking at me again. "Why?" she asked, as bewildered as any of us.

"I don't know why," I answered and it was true, I didn't. I'd never dealt with anything like this before. "I think whatever's there, it's bad. It's..." How could I say this? "It's pure evil."

"Pure evil?" Angus repeated. "Isn't that something of a conundrum?"

A wry laugh escaped me. Yes, I supposed it was. "What I'm trying to say is, I think it's some sort of—"

"Demon," Eilidh finished. Her voice, the kind of voice you hoped belonged to a woman such as her, petite, in her early to mid-sixties, and so very homely, no longer sounded soft and sweet. The solemnness in it echoed my own.

Even so, hearing her actually say the word, I backtracked. "I don't know whether it's a demon or a spirit. If it is a spirit, it's a very disturbed one. Eilidh, Angus, the history of that place, the 'real' history I mean, that only the islanders know, I have to find it out."

"Aye, lass, you will, you will," responded Eilidh, back to being homely again, "but not tonight. It's rest you need. Now come on, away to bed with you. I'll show you the way."

Rising from my chair, I started to follow her, but not before offering a still perplexed Angus another apologetic smile. Thankfully he smiled as well.

"Sleep well," he said.

"You too."

Upstairs, on the narrow landing, one that was bathed in the warm glow of a sixty-watt bulb, Eilidh stood in front of my room, smiling too. "I've put a glass of water by your bedside. If you'd like me to leave the landing light on tonight, that's fine, I can do that."

I shook my head. "It's okay; I don't mind the dark normally."

"Not you, no, but…" She stopped what she was saying and gave a little cough. "Well, you've a lamp in your room anyway, you can leave that on if you've a mind to."

"Thanks," I whispered, still staring at her as she turned and made her way back down the stairs.

I was curious. If it wasn't me that's afraid of the dark, who did she think might be?

Chapter Seven

STILL the images come. Even in sleep there's no escape. They're not as bad as when I was in Caitir's room, they're more diluted somehow and a part of me realises that I'm asleep – that this time it's a dream, not real at all, and that at some point I'll wake up. I'm trying so hard to wake up, to walk through the door that separates the world of dreams and reality, but every time I approach it, every time I get close, the door slams shut, traps me again.

I'm not going to be at the mercy of whatever's causing this. I refuse to be.

I remind myself what I have to do: imagine white light, pure and impenetrable.

Pure?

Hadn't I mentioned the word 'pure' earlier?

Pure evil.

Oh, the things I'd seen. Had Ally seen them too?

The things I was seeing…

Instruments of torture, ancient and rusted, forged in fire with the sole intention of causing pain. Agony, the screams and cries of all those that had ever been subjected to such instruments combining to form one single terrible sound that never faltered, that rang on and on and on. In the dream I hold my hands to my ears, attempting to drown that sound out, all the while knowing it's in vain. I fear for my sanity – such images have the power to destroy you, they can leave you a gibbering wreck confined to a white-padded cell for the rest of your life, they'd torment you, ceaselessly, in the lonely reaches of the night, and during daylight hours too. Was the light strong enough to combat this?

Of course it is! The light is all-powerful.

But do I believe that, do I really?

If only I didn't feel so alone.

You chose to be alone.

No, I didn't, not like this.

I've got to wake up. I have to. This dream is dangerous. This dream will… change me. I'm vulnerable whilst asleep. I'm a victim, waiting to be devoured, to be swallowed whole.

I have to reach the door, just as I did before, although there's no Angus to help me.

You attacked him!

Yes, I did, but I didn't mean to. I didn't even wholly re-alise… My hands just… struck out.

You lost control.

I shake my head. Control was taken from me – there's a difference.

The door, Ness, focus on the door. I'm trying to, but what waits on the other side? More darkness?

It's okay; I don't mind the dark normally.

I'd also said that earlier. Who to? A mother. Not my mother. My mother's dead.

Angus's mother!

Of course, I'm getting so confused. It's hard to think straight, to think at all.

I'm not afraid of the dark, but someone doesn't like it; Eilidh was right about that.

No, no, no, I can't think of her now. I mustn't.

But her voice is suddenly all I can hear.

Ness, Ness, is that you?

I must wake up.

Ness, I don't like the dark.

Pinching is supposed to wake a person up; I'll try pinching my hand.

You know how I hate it.

Pinching harder, I'm clawing at my skin.

My dark isn't like your dark. There are things in it.

My hand feels sticky. Why is that? Is it because I'm bleeding?

I can't see them, Ness, but I know they're there. Just because you can't see something, doesn't mean it doesn't exist. These things, they wander round, looking for someone to latch onto. They're relentless. They need constant feeding; they need nourishment.

There *is* blood; I'm covered in it. It's dripping onto the floor, surrounding me, so much of it. Not dripping, it's pouring.

If they see me, Ness, if they see you... Ness, please, don't leave me alone in the dark.

I have to wake up! I have to!

I'm going mad trying to hide from them. If I had a name, an identity, it might be different, but I've neither. So I'm lost too, as lost as they are. Ness, what's my name?

NESS!

Chapter Eight

SITTING at the dining table with the morning's post-storm light doing its utmost to brighten the room, my body is shaking as much as it ever did last night. Clearly this wasn't lost on Eilidh, who was busy setting three places for breakfast.

"There's no law against having a wee dram in the morning too, not in Scotland."

"What? Oh, Eilidh, I'm sorry… no thanks."

She waved her hand in the air. "Och, take no notice of me, I wasn't being serious. Now, what would you like for breakfast? I've sausage, a lovely bit of bacon, black pudding—"

"Oh God, no." I couldn't help but grimace – after the visions, and the dream too, with helpless people treated as nothing but meat, the blood there'd been, there's no way I'll be able to eat what she's offering. "I don't mean to be rude. It's not that I'm a vegetarian…"

Continuing to stare at me for a few moments, those grey-green eyes of hers so penetrating, her smile returned. "Scrambled eggs it is."

"Thank you," I muttered, intrigued again. It's as if she *knows* the details behind my refusal. She doesn't. She knows the bare minimum. If anything, she's *resisted* being told.

On her way into the kitchen, she bypassed Angus – his red hair as awry as ever, and matching the stubble on his jaw, which masked the bruise I inflicted at least.

"Morning," he sounded cheery enough. "Did you sleep well?"

I couldn't see the point in lying. "Not particularly."

"I thought not."

"Oh, how come?"

"I went to the bathroom in the night, to get some water. When I passed your room, you were… I'm not sure how to put it really… yelping."

"Yelping?"

"Aye," he continued, unabashed. "I did the decent thing and knocked on your door, obviously you didn't answer it, but it stopped the yelping anyway. Nightmare?"

"A nightmare? No, of course not, I yelp in my dreams for fun."

My sarcasm caused a burst of laughter. "That's all too easy to believe, I'm afraid."

I smiled also before lowering my eye. "That bruise on your chin—"

"Aye, aye, you can pack a punch for a wee 'un. Seriously though, it doesn't matter; I don't want you to fret about it anymore. Bruises fade."

Once again I tried to explain. "The visions were relentless. What was happening in them, I… it made me angry, really angry, I mean, which could be why I hit out."

He frowned. "You don't actually know?"

"Why I hit out? No, I don't, not for sure."

"A spirit can make you do that? It can possess you?"

"*If* it was a spirit."

"Oh aye, that's right, and not the devil himself."

"I wouldn't go that far," I said, struggling to smile this time.

His expression softened. "It's tough, what you do, isn't it?"

"Not always." And that was the truth; sometimes it was actually very straightforward.

He seemed to mull over my reply before answering. "I know I can't see what you can, but you're not alone. Not here anyway. Have you heard that the Scots are a fey race?"

My smile was a little wider this time. "I have, yes."

"Aye, well, it's true, some of us are. And those of us that aren't, well, we don't doubt our own people."

"But I'm not one of you," I pointed out.

"Aye, you're a Sassenach."

"A what?"

"A Lowlander, an English person."

I screwed up my nose. "Ah, I see, sorry about that."

"S'okay, not all the English are bad. We're quite fond of some of them." More seriously, he added, "What I'm trying to say is we won't doubt you either."

"Why?" I asked. In his own way, Angus was as intriguing as his mother.

He sat back in his chair and shrugged. "Because when you live here, in God's own country, it's hard to deny that there's something else out there." Slowly, he shook his head. "Up here, it's as if you're closer to something bigger, something good, sacred even."

"We're not talking about something sacred though."

"Aye, but good and bad go hand in hand sometimes, don't they?"

Before I could reply, Eilidh returned, two plates

55

containing eggs and toast in her hands.

"What's this?" Angus looked puzzled. "Is there none of that bacon left?"

"There's plenty."

"But—"

"Stop you're mithering, son, and eat whilst it's warm. You've a busy day ahead."

* * *

The weather may have cleared somewhat, but it was still a drizzly day, grey cloud concealing so much. Standing on Eilidh's doorstep with nothing but hills and sheep surrounding me, it was at once beautiful and oppressive.

"Cloud Island," muttered Angus, coming to stand beside me.

"Sorry?"

"The word Skye is Norse, it means Cloud Island, named for the whirling mists that you're admiring right now." He sighed. "It's as if this island wants to hide sometimes, to keep itself separate from the rest of the world, and, as I may have mentioned before, the people that live here are the same. Ness," he continued, an earnest look in his eyes, "whatever happens on Skye—"

"Stays on Skye. I know the saying."

"We're a private people. If there is something… *unnatural* happening, we'll be the ones to deal with it."

"Naturally," I said, smiling.

He smiled too. "With your help of course."

"A Sassenach?" I teased and then thought about it. "You know for a fey race, I'm surprised there's not a psychic amongst you."

56

"Maybe there is, but people only like to admit so much."

His words dismayed me. Even here, in God's own country, you couldn't be true to yourself – different *meant* different, whatever the location.

"So, what's on the agenda for today?" Angus asked. "Another trip to the lighthouse?"

"Not yet," I started walking towards his car, waiting patiently at the passenger door. "I'd really like to speak to Ally Dunn first, or at least her parents."

Angus didn't look too hopeful. "It might be best to build up to Ally Dunn. What about some of the other teenagers?"

"Let's try Ally," I persisted. "At least give it a go."

Having joined me at his car, Angus climbed into the driver's seat. "Aye, I suppose we could. I know Ally's parents well, I could pave the way."

"Do they know about me, why I'm here?"

"I haven't told them yet. A few of the other parents of the teenagers know though and they seem willing enough to have a word. Are you sure you don't want to try them first?"

In the seat beside him, I remained resolute. "I'd like to cut to the chase. There's only so long I can stay on Skye."

Smiling, he started the engine, which clunked loudly before springing into life. "You know there's those that come to Skye and never leave. They find it suits them here."

"And there are those that flee at the drop of a hat, remember?"

Again he burst out laughing. "Okay, Ally Dunn's it is. They live over near Dunvegan, just a few miles away."

It may have been just a few miles, but on Skye's winding

roads – that ribbon through the rise and fall of craggy rock, heather and sheep – the journey seemed to take forever, leaving me a little nauseous into the bargain. Similar had happened yesterday when Angus had picked me up from Inverness Airport. We'd then driven seventy miles across some of the most amazing terrain I'd ever seen before taking the car ferry over Loch Alsh to reach the island. Our journey far from over, it was another fifty-something miles to the township of Glendale, where he and his mother lived, more magnificent views at my disposal, particularly the brooding Cuillin Mountains capped in tumbling cloud, which held me spellbound. But those twisting, turning lanes, they were something to be endured. By the time we'd reached Eilidh's, I was feeling a little worse for wear as well as extremely tired – not the best state in which to kick-start a psychic investigation in hindsight.

During that same drive, the conversation between us had been slightly stilted; as well it might be considering we were two strangers meeting for the first time. I'd also deliberately refrained from asking too much about Minch Point Lighthouse, at least until I'd actually set foot in the place, not wanting to encourage preconceptions, but now it was different, I *had* to know more and this journey was as good a time as any to pump Angus for information.

He replied knowledgeably enough, but it was the more technical details he was familiar with: that it was first lit in July 1909, that the tower itself is 43 metres tall, and the light – when it had been working – could be seen from twenty-four miles distance. There was also a foghorn, but that was disabled now too. It was just an empty building, falling into disrepair.

"And through the years, as far as you know, Angus,

various keepers have lived there without incident?"

He glanced briefly at me. "Aye, right up until the Camerons."

"Are any of those that lived there still on the island?"

He shook his head. "The lighthouse keeper before Cameron was Donder McKendrick. He retired to the mainland, near Inverness I think, a good while ago. Went to be closer to his daughter. My mother knew him and his wife, nice enough people apparently."

"It might be necessary to pay him a visit."

"If he's still alive," Angus began and then paused, trying hard to suppress a smirk. "Not that that's strictly necessary for you, is it?"

His teasing was good-natured enough. "Believe me, if they're alive, it's easier."

His voice grew more serious. "You know, Mum and me, we're happy for you to stay as long as you like. I know it's not a big house, but hopefully you're finding it comfortable."

"It's very comfortable, thanks." And it was – a traditional white house, as so many of them were on Skye, with a slate roof. It was warm and cosy, and in it I was made to feel at home rather than a jobbing visitor. Only Angus and his mother lived there, his father having died a couple of years before, his spirit not lingering I was glad to note, only a sense of his beloved presence. "But I do have other work to get back to."

"With the police you mean?"

I nodded. "I also work for Brighton Council on an *ad hoc* basis."

"They need a psychic too?"

"Not every tenant pays rent."

He bellowed with laughter. "I think I've heard it all now, the local council involved in spirit eviction! Your work with the police though, that must be interesting at times."

"At times."

He must have caught the more sombre note in my voice as he turned to look at me more fully. "Do you get results?" he asked.

"Mostly… Angus, watch the road will you, there's a car coming."

The car was actually a fair distance away, nonetheless I was glad of the excuse it gave me to cut Angus off.

We passed the road sign for Dunvegan. "Does Ally live in the village?"

"A wee bit on the outskirts. We're not far now, another mile or two."

The drizzle had become rain, the clouds even lower than before, and the sheep at the side of the road looking sodden and forlorn. Desolate was the word that sprang to mind as I peered outwards at the grey, barren scree slopes. If it was beautiful, it was a melancholy beauty. This was a land that was hard to live in; I'm not sure I'd be able to. A land in lockdown for many months, enslaved by the elements. In it, some things would never be able to prosper. Other things, however, would prosper well enough.

"That's the Dunns' house," announced Angus, "right up ahead."

It was another white house, but one that wasn't as pristine as Eilidh's, the patch of garden that surrounded it once neat perhaps, but which had clearly been left to its own devices recently with grass left wild and the weeds running riot. There were five windows at the front, two downstairs and three above in the eaves. At every one of the windows the curtains were closed, despite it being close to eleven on a weekday morning. As Angus stopped the car and we approached the front door on foot, I could feel the unease in the air. I should think anyone could.

I turned to Angus. "Are you okay?"

"Aye, I'm fine," he replied, but I could tell from his slightly worried expression that I was right, he could feel it too – a cloud of another kind that hung over the house.

While Angus rang the doorbell, I hugged the obsidian in my pocket.

Chapter Nine

"ANGUS Macbrae, what can I do for you?"

"Molly, hello, I've…erm… That is *we've* come to see you and John, to talk about Ally."

Molly Dunn raised an eyebrow as she shifted her gaze from Angus to me, clearly unimpressed with this intrusion. "Exactly who does 'we' consist of?"

"I'm Vanessa Patterson," I said, smiling as I held my hand out. "If we could come inside, I can explain who I am and what I'm doing here."

She seemed appalled at the idea. "You can't come in. It's… it's… not a good time."

"Molly," I persevered, "I don't think it's been a good time for the last two months, has it?"

"What? I…" At once her resolve broke and her face, far too haggard for someone of around forty, fell into an expression of despair. "How do you know that?" she whispered. "What's Angus been saying?"

"Only the truth," I assured her.

"She works with the police," Angus blurted out.

Molly's pale eyes widened, "You're a detective?"

I bit down on any retort I might have had for Angus and admitted what I was, there and then, on the doorstep. "I'm a psychic. That's the capacity in which I work for the police."

"This is *not* a police matter," she growled, her nostrils flaring slightly.

"I know, I know… Look, if I could come in, I can explain."

"John isn't at home."

"Then perhaps we can talk to you first, Molly? Please."

I'm not sure I would have pushed so hard if I hadn't sensed quite how desperate she was, that this entire matter was. Something was building, but what climax it was rushing towards I still had no idea. Nor how much time was left before it peaked.

"Molly," I continued. "We just need to talk."

Perhaps she sensed how desperate I was too, as she stared at me for only a few more seconds before dropping her gaze and standing aside. Glancing briefly at Angus, who nodded, I sidled past her and down a narrow hallway.

"Turn right," she instructed, "into the living room."

A pleasant enough room, despite the darkness, there was no sign of Ally; maybe she was upstairs in her bedroom. Tilting my head, I noticed a spider web crack in the ceiling, just as there'd been in the living room ceiling at the lighthouse.

Molly and Angus followed me into the room, Molly indicating for us to take a seat. Her eyes kept flickering upwards, as her teeth agitated at an already sore lip.

"The curtains," I said, feeling the need for some light, however pitiful.

"She doesn't like me to open them."

"Ally?"

A sharp nod was her only reply.

"Angus has briefed me on what happened that night at

the lighthouse—"

"Briefed you? You said you weren't a detective."

"I'm not, I'm sorry, he's *told* me what happened."

"What he knows of it," she corrected.

"That's right. Perhaps you can tell me what's been happening since."

I could feel how tense Angus was beside me and wished I'd come alone so I wouldn't have to worry about him. But then it was only because of him that I'd managed to gain entry into the Dunn household at all, and so decided to be grateful, although the police angle he was promoting, I'd have to have a word with him about that. Police, psychics; neither were popular. The last thing I needed was a double whammy of distrust.

"Molly?" I prompted when she fell silent.

"It's difficult," she whispered, her eyes again flickering upwards.

"If it's possible I'd like to talk to Ally too at some point."

"Ha! Good luck with that! She hardly talks to anyone anymore, not even me."

I seized the moment. "What does she do?"

"She sits, that's all, and stares at the wall. She hardly eats, hardly drinks, and there's no hope of getting her to school. The teachers are being very good, they provide me with material to home school her, and I do, I sit and I read through everything with her, but she barely acknowledges me. Their patience is going to run out soon."

"And your patience?" I ask.

"Mine? I'm her mother!"

She'd taken offence, but I ignored that. "Molly, as her mother, this is the hardest of all for you. Has she said

64

anything at all about what happened at the lighthouse?"

"Nothing. But when she sleeps, she dreams, and when she dreams, she mutters. She sounds frightened, as if she's trying to escape something. Sometimes she lifts her hands and bats at something above her, turning her head from side to side and yelping."

At the use of that word, I sensed Angus looking at me – he'd said I'd been yelping too last night. I ignored him, my entire attention on Molly. "Go on," I said.

"I woke her once, during one of these dreams, and she lashed out at me." Her voice was trembling as much as her body. "John heard the commotion and came running. He had to pull her off me. Oh my girl, my poor wee pet, it's awful, just awful."

Her words ended on a sob, one that galvanised Angus into action. He jumped up to stand awkwardly by her side. "Will I get you a cup of tea, Molly?"

"No, no." She waved her hand at him. "Tea won't help. *Nothing* helps." Wiping at her eyes, she lifted her head to stare at me again. "Whatever happened at the lighthouse, it was bad, very bad. I keep thinking she might be… that's she's…"

She didn't have to say it, I knew what she meant – possessed. I hoped not, but I couldn't deny it either, not until I'd talked to Ally. If she was possessed, what by? It could still be a spirit. I'd heard of such things happening before, but not encountered it personally. If it was something non-spirit… I swallowed. Was I out of my depth here?

A loud thud from upstairs captured our attention.

"Is that Ally?" I asked.

Molly nodded. "Her bedroom's just above."

"The cracks in the ceiling…?"

"They weren't there before," she admitted. "As much as John and I are frustrated, Ally is too, I think. There are times when she barricades herself in, and when she does, it's as if she's hurling herself from wall to wall in some mad frenzy. I've shouted through the door, I've pleaded with her to stop, but she won't. And she can keep it going for ages. The screams and the yells, it's heart-breaking to hear, truly heart-breaking. Before this, she was so lovely; she was bright, funny, and sociable. She was our angel."

Molly was crying again, sobbing, Angus still hovering uncertainly by, feeling just as bad as I did. More than ever I had to get to the bottom of what was happening. My gift could go some way towards enabling me, and so I had to use it accordingly.

There was one more thing I needed to know before I headed upstairs.

"Have the church been involved in what's happening here?"

"We're not church-goers," she replied. "It's not that we don't believe, but we've never been regulars. The Reverend Drummond is the minister at our local church and he's itching to get involved. I know it. He's heard rumours, you see, people love to gossip around here, you can't escape it. But I don't want the church involved, the police, or any of the authorities, I don't want them thinking that we've done something wrong, that all of this is our fault. It isn't. We're good parents. We've done our best by her. We love her, so much. I can't fob the school off for much longer though. They'll be the ones to involve others, I know it. And if that happens, if she's taken away from us…"

"Molly, I'm not the authorities, I'm just a person who thinks I can help."

"Because you're psychic?"

"Because I have a connection with the other side, because I can see."

She sniffed and blew her nose on a tissue that Angus had handed her. "And you won't breathe a word of this to the police, to Reverend Drummond either? You won't take this off-island? You have to promise me, mind. You have to say it."

"I promise."

She settled back in the armchair, confusion, wariness and hope battling inside her – hope eventually winning out.

"Then go upstairs," she said, her voice a mere whisper. "See what you can do."

* * *

Angus wanted to come with me, but I insisted he stayed with Molly, get her that cup of tea after all, and to make sure there was sugar in it. He was reluctant but he agreed.

"I'm here if you need me, just… shout or something, and I'll come running."

"Thanks," I said, appreciating his concern.

Leaving them, I stood at the bottom of the stairs staring upwards. It was dark up there, with no light allowed to infiltrate. I had such an urge to rush around and start drawing the curtains back, but if I wasn't given permission to do that, it was an urge I had to dampen.

I climbed one step at a time. It was like wading through treacle. How could the Dunns stand it? The atmosphere, charged as it was with fear and bewilderment, was utterly depressing. No wonder Molly – let alone Ally – was in such a state. At least the husband could escape during the day, thanks to his work, but the prospect of returning here, night after night… I'm not sure I could do it.

Either side of me, on the walls, were framed pictures, a huge variety of them, all of them validating what Molly had said, that they were a happy family, or had once been. Staring at them gave me a chance to get to know what Ally looked like, although it was Ally through the ages that they depicted, as a sweet baby, a cute toddler, Ally at a slightly awkward pre-teen age and as a full-blown teenager, but still smiling, still laughing alongside her parents. She was sixteen now – an only child – a *treasured* only child. How wonderful that must have felt. How terrible for it to have gone awry.

Leaving her bright youthful face behind, I reached the landing, turning in the direction of her bedroom. God, I wished they'd let the light in – it really would help. I'm not afraid to admit, I felt scared. I felt vulnerable and alone too. What was it that I was going to encounter in that lair of hers? Not the smiling Ally that filled my mind, that was for certain.

Refusing to think, determined to act, I forced one foot in front of the other. The closer I got, the denser the atmosphere became. Once again my breathing became erratic and I had to stop several times to force myself to inhale to a count of four and exhale for the same amount. My heartbeat steadier, I positioned myself in front of her door and knocked.

As I expected there was no reply.

"Ally, my name's Vanessa Patterson, I've come to talk to you about what's been happening lately, about how you've been feeling. I'm not here in any official capacity, please don't worry about that, I'm here as someone who wants to help. You've nothing to fear from me, nothing at all." As with the dead, initially my job was all about cajoling.

Once more I was ignored, so I decided to force the issue and twisted the handle. Molly said that Ally barricaded herself in during more troubled times, I was glad to note that this wasn't one of them as the door yielded easily enough. I entered, my eyes searching for her in the darkness. There she was, sitting on a chair by the window, not staring out of it, but staring at the closed curtains, so still that for a moment I gave in to panic. "Ally, are you okay?"

The slightest of movements reassured me she was still alive, and that she could hear me well enough. Although instinct screamed at me to leave the door open, and therefore the path to escape clear, I closed it, thinking that in her current state she might prefer it.

"Ally," I said again, edging my way over to the bed and sitting close to where she was. "I should come clean about who I really am. I'm a psychic. Do you know what that means? Shall I explain?" When there was no answer, I did just that, wondering if that at least might provoke a reaction. It didn't. She was statue-like.

I looked around her room, took it all in. Only the bed was unmade, otherwise it was fairly neat and tidy, Molly steadfastly refusing to let her daughter reside in squalor – picking clothes up if they were left on the floor, changing sheets, polishing surfaces, vacuuming. I could see her now, in my mind's eye, carrying out such mundane tasks, and all in the darkness. The walls, which Ally would hurl herself against on occasion, may well be scuffed, but it was impossible to tell without the light on. I inhaled. There was no stale sweat, no smell of grime. What there was, was an underlying sweetness – the same unpleasantness to it as the smell at the lighthouse – a *connection*.

"Ally, what happened? Tell me. Whatever you say, I'll believe you, no matter how outlandish you might think it is, how crazy or weird. I'm on your side."

I have a good amount of patience, you need it in my job, but there were also times when you have to make a judgement call. It was time to explain further.

"Ally, I've been to the lighthouse too, last night. I went up to Caitir's room, where you and your friends played Thirteen Ghost Stories. I sensed there was something there."

At last a response – a mumble that I couldn't quite hear.

"Sorry, Ally, could you repeat that?"

"Did you play the game?"

Her voice was croaky, as if her throat had become as rusty with disuse as the pipes at Minch Point. "No, I didn't play the game, but I tuned in, and I had an experience too."

No verbal reply this time, but she did turn her head further towards me. I was able to study her profile a little better, a pretty girl, or she would be if she didn't look so strained – even in the darkness I could tell that. She was as worn as her mother. What should I do? Describe what I'd seen? I'd have to, but a significantly watered-down version. The last thing I wanted was to remind her of how vicious the visions had been.

"Ally, as I was leaving Caitir's room, images started to fill my mind, they came in rapid succession, one after the other, like a movie reel. These visions…" I paused. It's not as if I wanted reminding either. "They were… nasty. Very. Did you see something too?"

She issued another mumble, forcing me to lean closer to hear what she was saying.

"Animals, cats, my favourite, dogs too, blood, hurt, all of them. So much blood."

I shuddered at her words. "I know."

"Kids, younger than me. Kids my age too. Friends. Screaming. Crying."

And not just that, there was also the pleading, the begging, and the sheer lack of any mercy shown. It seems we *had* seen similar visions, and once seen, how could we forget? I wanted to bleach my mind, to scrub away the scars they'd left, but it was impossible. Such sights destroyed innocence. They left you feeling corrupted. No wonder Ally was suffering. But there had to be a way back – for both of us.

"Ally, whatever you saw, it's important to remember that it's over now. The images, the horror will fade with time. Here's what I do: whenever I remember, I replace it with another image, with something positive, something I love. You could try and do that too. Keep pushing the negative away, until eventually it recedes, and loses its power. Right now, what we've seen is holding us in its thrall, it's making us afraid and we can't afford to be. Fear is what keeps negativity thriving." When she failed to answer me, I dared to do something: I reached out and touched her shoulder. Inwardly I gasped. She was so cold, despite it being warm enough in the room, like a carving made from ice. "Ally, listen to me, please, you're not alone with this, I'm here now. Together we'll beat it."

"What do you love?"

I retracted my hand. "I'm sorry?"

She turned more fully, dark hollows for eyes giving her a

ghoulish look. "What do you love?"

"I… erm… love lots of things. I love…" Damn it, but I had to struggle to answer this surprising question. "Chocolate." A small laugh escaped me, one with a nervous edge to it. "Doesn't everyone? A cup of tea with milk and one sugar; I love films; I love reading. One of my favourite books used to be *Jane Eyre* by Charlotte Brontë. Have you read it? I love animals, all animals really, no favourites there. I used to knit. Not so much anymore, but when I was younger. It helped me to focus somehow and having something nice to wear as a result of it was an added bonus. I—"

Those hollow eyes met mine. "*Who* do you love?"

Her voice sounded croakier than ever, scratchy almost

"W…who?" I repeated, stumbling slightly over the word.

"Who do you love?" She was glaring at me now.

"I… I love…"

"Who?"

"I…"

"WHO?"

"Stop yelling, Ally, stop demanding. That will get us nowhere."

She thrust her face forward, such a sudden action that I couldn't help but be alarmed by it. "Who do you love?"

Quickly I gathered myself. "Ally, this isn't you speaking. I think what's happening—"

"Your brothers?"

Again I was taken aback. "My brothers? Yes, yes of course."

"Liar!"

"Ally, whatever's in you is trying to take control."

"Your sisters?"

"Yes, Ally, I love my sisters. I do."

"Liar!"

I started to rise, but my legs felt like lead. *Get a grip, Ness, get a grip.*

"Your father?"

My breathing, I couldn't keep it steady anymore. "Ally, I'm warning you, I won't listen to any more—"

"Your mother?" At that a sly smile spread across her face. "Do you love your mother?"

I was able to stand at last. Ally knew nothing about my family, and nor did whatever it was that had hold of her. Towering over her as she sat in her chair, seemingly relaxed, casual even, I did my utmost to rein in the feelings – the memories – that were trying to overwhelm me, as horrific, *personally* horrific, as any of the visions I'd had at the lighthouse. "Ally, I know you're in there. Fight this thing. Don't be afraid."

She laughed – a cackle that didn't belong to her, but to something far more ancient. "I'm not afraid, you are. You're terrified. And your weak spot, I've found it."

"Leave my family out of this."

Ally refused to obey. "Your poor mother, what a torment you were to her."

"I've told you, I won't listen."

"This thing she'd spawned, as terrible as I am, an abomination. How it hurt her."

As I'd forced my legs towards Ally's room, I now had to force them to move away, from her and from the darkness that clung to her. But shock had rendered me slow.

"You drove her to an early grave."

How far the door was – an ocean of carpet separating us.

73

"You hurt your twin too, so bad."

Thrusting my hands out, I imagined a rope in front of me, and someone at the end of it; a friend, not a foe, hauling me towards the door. I had to go and come back stronger.

Stronger? What a joke! I'd never felt so weak.

"Remember, Ness, how you hated them."

Reaching my goal, I could barely see for the tears in my eyes. If I expected the door to be stuck again, it wasn't. It opened and I fled, but not before Ally issued her last words.

"And remember this: they hated you too."

Chapter Ten

1974

WHAT'S wrong with Mum?

I shrugged. "Don't know. Don't care."

She's being sick all the time.

"I told you, I don't know. How would I? She barely speaks to me."

Well, something's wrong.

I ignored my twin and her concerns, and continued to read my book – I got through so many, confined as I was to my bedroom, by choice as much as anything. Today, I was alone in the house with Mum. My father was at work, and my brothers and sisters were either at work too or school. I wasn't at school because I had a stuffed-up nose, a headache, a sore throat and blocked ears. Normally I never missed a day even when I wasn't feeling well. Mum always insisted I went. But, when I'd gone into her room to complain how I felt this morning, she'd just waved her hand at me, and said it was fine, that I could go back to bed. I couldn't believe my luck. I hadn't questioned it, hadn't hung around for a minute longer than necessary in case she had a change of heart, I'd simply raced out of her room and back into mine, closing the door behind me.

I had a whole day to myself – no teachers, and no one to

ignore me in the playground. Bliss! I could read to my heart's content, do some colouring in, sleep even. I really did feel ill. What would have made it perfect was if my twin had kept away too. Some days she did, but today was unfortunately not one of them. She was worried about Mum and to be honest, I was a little bit too. I could hear her in the bathroom retching; it was a horrible, gurgling sound. As much as I tried to focus on my book, I couldn't. She'd shown some mercy towards me earlier, perhaps I should go and show some sympathy towards her.

I looked at the shadow of my twin, thought I saw her nod in approval.

"Okay, okay, I'm going," I said, shutting my book perhaps a little too hard. It was *Jane Eyre* – the story of another lonely girl – and I was really enjoying it, although the last chapter I'd read, where poor Jane had been locked in the Red Room by the terrible Mrs Reed had left me somewhat reeling. Leaving my room, I tentatively made my way to the bathroom and knocked on the door. Rather than vomiting, Mum seemed to be groaning, as if she were in considerable pain.

"Mum, it's me. Are you okay?" Stupid question really, but still I asked it. "Mum, do you want me to get you a glass of water?" Another stupid question, she was in a bathroom for goodness' sake, there was water enough in there! "Mum, say something. Please."

My twin was by my side. *Try the handle; see if the door will open.*

It did, something that caused both fear and more trepidation.

Taking a deep breath, I entered the bathroom. The first thing I saw was blood – *the red room* – the tiles, normally a pale grey, were covered in it.

My hand flew to my mouth. "Oh God, Mum! Are you dying?"

Despite everything, that realisation was shocking. I was a child – I couldn't lose my mother! Terror drove me forward. "Mum, it's okay, I'm here. Tell me what to do."

She was slumped on the floor, her head resting against the side of the bath. Doll-like, her face was pale and waxy and her arms hung limp by her side. Not caring about the blood, I knelt beside her and reached out.

"Don't touch me!"

Her words stopped me in mid-action. "Mum!" I implored.

"Call your father."

Lowering my hands, I nodded. "What shall I tell him?"

"The baby…" her voice was low, guttural even, "…the baby's dead."

"Another one?" I gasped. I couldn't help myself.

"Yes!" she spat. "Another one."

I swallowed. "Ambulance," I muttered. "I'll call an ambulance."

"CALL YOUR FATHER!"

I pushed myself away from her, stood up and ran from the room, slipping on the bloodied floor as I went, crashing onto the landing, leaving footprints behind me on the oatmeal coloured carpet. Once downstairs, I dialled my father's office number with trembling fingers – it took three attempts before I made a connection. When he answered, I told him as best I could what was happening. He kept telling me to slow down, but I couldn't. Finally, he told me to go back upstairs, to stay with mum, that he was on his way, and would be there as soon as possible. I think

I heard him swear as he replaced the receiver.

At the bottom of the stairwell, I stopped. I didn't want to go back up there. What was the point? She didn't want my help. I had to though; Dad had said so.

Once more in the bathroom, I saw that Mum had tried to straighten herself up, saw too how wet her cheeks were, and the tears that glistened there. She was sobbing, snot running from her nose, which she wiped at with the back of her hand.

"I'm sorry, Mum." I didn't know what else to say.

"Probably just as well," she managed.

I frowned. What did she mean?

"Like you. If it was like you."

"Like me?"

"Wrong! All wrong."

I took a step back, not sure if I could bear to hear what she was going to say. Not again.

She continued to mutter. "No more of this, I want no more. My luck ran out with you."

Tears blinded me too. "Mum, don't. Please don't."

But she was in her stride.

"I believe in Jesus, Mary and Joseph. I believe in God. It's what normal people believe in, self-respecting people. I *don't* believe this world is full of ghosts, of people long gone, that they walk alongside us, that they try and communicate, that they're lost somehow, that they need our help. It's not true, none of it. You're a liar, and you always have been. You just make it all up. I don't believe I'm capable of producing something like you."

She'd said *something* this time, not even *someone*. Anger overtook despair. "But you did though," I replied, shaking with the injustice of it all. "You produced two of us."

"DON'T YOU DARE TALK ABOUT WHAT HAPPENED!"

I could see my twin. She was standing beside my mother, staring down at her, with such sadness in her expression. "Look," I said, lifting my hand to point. "She's there right now, my twin sister, she's standing beside you and your words, they're hurting her too."

"The filth that comes out of your mouth."

"It's true! Look up. Can't you see her? Can't you sense her? Look at where I'm pointing!"

I don't know if it was something in my voice, a thread of steel perhaps, but she obeyed and for a moment, a brief moment, I thought I saw her eyes widen.

"You *can* see her, can't you? What's her name, Mum? What did you call her? She wants to know so badly."

Slowly, very slowly, my Mum turned back. Her voice when she spoke was loaded.

"I will continue to clothe you, I will continue to feed you. I will do my duty, as the state requires. But the minute you're old enough, you leave. Do you hear? I want you gone."

All anger, all defiance spent, despair engulfed me yet again.

I took another step back and then fled from the room, leaving my mother, my twin, and another sibling who'd never live in this world, but who hadn't lingered at least; who'd had the good sense to fly back to where he or she had come from: a better place than this.

Because this – my home – was nothing less than perdition.

Chapter Eleven

"ANOTHER cup of tea, Ness?"

"No thanks, Angus. I'm done now, I'm okay."

"You sure? You still look really pale."

"I *am* pale," I replied, smiling a little. "My skin never seems to tan, not even in the height of summer. Seriously, I'm fine. It's just... I've things on my mind lately."

"The mystery of the lighthouse?"

"That's certainly one of them."

Having escaped Ally, I'd managed to pull myself together, heading downstairs, past all those smiling photographs of the perfect family, ignoring every one of them, using the time I had to compose myself instead. The last thing I wanted was to burst into the living room looking as shaky as I felt. Ally wasn't to be blamed for what had happened, she was an innocent being used as a pawn. Molly was, of course, curious as to how I'd got on.

"I need to find out more about the lighthouse," I'd said to her, "speak to other parents of the teenagers involved, get a more rounded picture of what happened." I hadn't looked at Angus when I said that, I was too embarrassed. That had been his suggestion after all.

"And then what?" she'd asked.

"Then I perform a cleansing."

"An exorcism?"

That wasn't a word I tended to use. "A cleansing is more of an holistic approach," I explained. "I'll use light and love to combat whatever it is that hides at the lighthouse."

She'd frowned at that, not as impressed, I suspected, than she would have been if I'd admitted to an exorcism. I explained further than it was the Catholic Church that tended to carry out exorcisms and if she didn't want the church involved, the authorities…

"Okay, okay," she said. "I understand what you're trying to say. But this cleansing, is it as effective?"

"It has been in the past." And it was true, but no two cases were ever the same. People were unique, so were spirits.

Having said goodbye to her and climbed back into Angus's car, my façade crumbled, tears stung my eyes as I screwed them shut. As he'd been when Molly had got upset, Angus was all concern. "What's wrong? Come on. Come here. You need a hug."

How much I needed it he'd never know.

Once he released me, I dried my eyes and he'd driven us to this café, a short way from Ally Dunn's house, and plied me with tea, brushing aside any apologies I might have.

"Right," he said, watching me as I pushed my cup away. "Is it the lighthouse you want to go to next or to see a few more parents?"

"Not the lighthouse, not today." I needed to be more stable than this before I returned there. "Let's piece together what we know already, and try and make some sense of it."

"Sounds like a plan," Angus agreed.

"Angus," I said, worried suddenly. "Are you okay to help me? I don't mean to sound rude or anything, I'm grateful for your help, but don't you have a job to go to?"

His face fell slightly. "Actually no, not right now. You could say I'm in between jobs."

"What did you do?" I asked. "And what are you going to be doing?"

"I was working in an architect's office, in Edinburgh actually, as an architectural technician. But it's not my true calling. Uncle Glenn said I could manage Minch Point when it's a guesthouse. I like meeting people, I like being on Skye. I thought I'd give it a whirl. To be honest, I couldn't wait to ditch my job. "

"So you've a vested interest in this case too?"

"Aye, well, yes, I do now. I'm counting on it. I'd like there to be a steady stream of guests, but also, I don't want the lighthouse to suffer from an ill reputation any more than my uncle does. We'd be finished before we even got started. For my uncle it's an investment opportunity, but for me it's much more than that."

"I wish you all the luck."

He smiled. "I wish us *both* luck."

My smile was a little more strained. "Okay, back to basics. We know that the Camerons lived at the lighthouse, that they abandoned it a decade ago, that it's been used as a playground for kids ever since, and that those kids, including you at one point, played a game there: Thirteen Ghost Stories. It's become something of a ritual."

"All correct," Angus replied.

"Around two months ago whilst playing the game, Ally Dunn, and even a few of the others, experienced something. They've been different ever since."

"Aye, the others are more subdued, but they still manage to get up, go to school and socialise to an extent. It's Ally that's been affected the most."

"I wonder why that is?"

"I don't know."

"And none of them have been back since?"

"Not that I know of." He paused. "Ness, what happened when you went to see Ally? You haven't really said."

"It's not easy seeing a kid so distressed, you know," I replied, palming him off a little.

"I understand that. But did she say anything... you know... to upset you?"

This man, was he as fey as his mother?

"No, it's fine. It's just... A lot of negative energy clings to Ally, it can have an effect."

"Oh aye, I'm sure," he conceded, nodding gravely.

"We also know that whilst the cabin boy, Liam, moved away soon after his dismissal, his father, Ron McCarron, lives here still and, despite what you said about finding him sober, I'm going to need to speak to him, see if there's any way I can contact Liam."

Angus didn't look too sure. "It's a long time ago that Liam worked for the Camerons."

"That's as maybe, but he lived there, alongside them, at the lighthouse, he'll have more of an insight than anyone."

"Aye, I suppose. It's worth a shot."

Anything was at this particular point in time, because whatever was happening in this corner of Skye, it wasn't getting any better.

* * *

The afternoon was spent visiting the parents of Isabel Croft, Craig Ludmore, and Grant MacIver. Considering prior arrangements to do so were hastily made by Angus via a phone call, we were greeted amicably enough, even keenly I'd say, certainly by Isabel's mother and Grant's father. When we were ushered into various living rooms, the story was the same – their children, all of whom were still at school during our visit – were much quieter than usual, they'd lost their spark, their zest, they were more nervy instead, jumping at anything and everything. Isabel's mother, Beth, had also found sheets of A4 paper in her daughter's room, reams of them, the number thirteen in-scribed on every inch of space, the paper jagged in places where she'd gripped the pen so hard.

"She'd hidden these sheets of paper," Beth explained as Angus and I sat on her sofa, "on top of her wardrobe, in her wardrobe, under her bed. Why would she do that?"

"Did you ask her why?" Angus enquired.

She shook her head as if the thought had never occurred to her. "No, no, I didn't. I suppose I felt... it would upset her somehow. I put them back where I found them. She's added to the pile since, there'll be no room for anything else in her room at this rate."

Grant's father told us how, when his son came home from school, he shut himself away in his room, only emerging to grab dinner and use the bathroom.

"At least he goes to school," Angus tried to soothe.

"Aye, that he does. But he used to be a sociable lad, sit-ting with his family in the evening, telling us all about his day, and what he's been up to. I miss him you know. We used to go fishing together at the weekend. Suddenly he doesn't want to do that either."

"It could be just a teenage thing," I venture.

"He's been a teenager for a while now," was Mr

MacIver's reply. "As I said, this is a sudden change, ever since that business at the lighthouse."

"It's an odd place," Craig's father told us when we visited his house. "You know about the shipwreck, don't you, which happened soon after the lighthouse was built?"

Angus nodded. "You think it's relevant?"

"I never used to, but I'm beginning to wonder."

"Mr Ludmore," I asked. "What happened exactly? Did many people die?"

"Oh aye," he said, "all those on board. Thirty-six to be precise, the bodies that were recovered either sent home or buried here on the island. I think the youngest deckhand was recorded as being no more than thirteen. A tragedy it was, and no matter that it was so long ago, the weight of that tragedy remains. The lens, a Fresnel lens too, supposedly one of the best – it either failed that night or the clouds were just too thick for the beam to penetrate, no one knows for sure. It's not a great beginning for a new lighthouse, is it?"

It wasn't – it was dreadful. "Any other shipwrecks of note?"

Mr Ludmore shook his head. "A few incidents, but no more deaths."

Mrs Ludmore, who'd been in the kitchen, came in to join us, a laden tray in her hands. "You talking about the shipwreck, Alan?" She exhaled heavily as she put the tray on the table in front of us and began to pour into china cups. "The blue men at work again."

I was lost. "The blue men?"

"Aye," she said, handing me a cup, "the blue men. Storm kelpies, in other words. It's said they inhabit the waters around here, playing havoc with sailors, and causing boats to overturn. There've been several people who've sworn blind that they've seen them in the past, when the weather's fine, just floating on the surface, sleeping. But they can conjure storms too, whenever the mood takes them, when they want fresh bodies to feast on."

"Och, Meg, away with you!" chided Mr Ludmore. Looking at me, he shrugged as if in apology for his wife's flight of fancy. "It's a myth that's all, but aye, there's many around here that believe in the blue men well enough."

"Belief is a powerful thing," I said. And perhaps not to be dismissed, nor all this talk of conjuring. Certainly something had been conjured at the lighthouse, perhaps feeding off any negative energy that remained from so many deaths – thirty-six of them and the youngest victim only thirteen. That number, how it kept recurring.

"Is the boy buried locally, the lad who died because of the shipwreck, do you know?"

"Aye," Mr Ludmore answered, "he's got a headstone at Kilchoan Cemetery, in Glendale. Angus, you must know it? It's in your neck of the woods."

"Aye, I know it."

"Perhaps we can stop off there on our way home?" I asked Angus.

"Of course, if you want to."

I did, I planned to touch his gravestone and see what I could glean from it.

Still on such a delicate subject, I remembered something I'd asked Angus the previous day, to which I hadn't yet got an answer. "Aside from the shipwreck, have there been any more known deaths at the lighthouse? In more modern times perhaps?"

Mr and Mrs Ludmore looked at each other and then at

me. "Are we talking murder here?" Mr Ludmore said.

I inclined my head a little. "Not necessarily."

"There's been no more deaths that I know of," he replied.

"Not at the lighthouse anyway," Mrs Ludmore added. "But there was another death. What was it, three or four years after the Camerons left. Not murder but not natural either."

My ears pricked up. "Oh?"

"A few miles from the lighthouse, following the coastline to the north, it was to do with a young girl. She threw herself from the cliffs, committed suicide in other words."

"How old was she?"

"Young, not even twenty."

"Do you know why she did it?"

"Not even her parents knew that. They were devastated, moved away soon after, wanting a fresh start, I should imagine. The one thing they did say was that she'd changed, and that that change had been quite sudden. She'd become moody and withdrawn, had stopped communicating with them. The lighthouse was empty by then, as you know, I'm wondering if she went there with her friends too, if something happened to her like it did to Ally, and to our kids. Oh God," her eyes widened, as her hand flew to her chest. "I've only really just put two and two together. What if, what if—"

Mr Ludmore immediately tried to soothe his wife. "No child of ours is going down the same route, don't worry yourself, lass. Don't even *think* it. And that girl, Moira her name was, she was a wild one. Och, I know her parents thought she was meek and mild, but come on, love, you know as well as I did that she had a reputation. She'd been giving them cause for concern for a long time, it didn't happen as suddenly as they claimed."

Angus broke into the conversation. "We shouldn't speak ill of the dead. Moira, she was… She was all right."

I turned to look at him. "You knew her?"

"Aye, I was a kid, barely sixteen when she died. Hung about with her sometimes in a big group, not that she ever noticed me." He paused and gave a wry laugh. "You couldn't help but notice her though. She was beautiful with long blonde hair, a tinkling laugh, and eyes that would sparkle." He fell into a silence, and not just any silence, it was mournful.

Gently I probed further. "Angus, did you hang about with her at the lighthouse?"

"On one or two occasions. Moira wasn't long into drugs before she died. They weren't easy to get hold of back then, not here, not on Skye, but there were rumours that she was dabbling, that somehow she'd found a supplier."

"Do you know what kind of drugs?"

"Again it was rumour, but I did hear mention of LSD."

I was surprised. "Wasn't LSD out of fashion by then? Heroin's more popular now."

"Scotland isn't like the rest of the UK," was his answer. "I heard it was LSD."

"Okay," I conceded. "When you were with her, did you ever suspect she was high?"

He shook his head. "No. Whatever she did, she didn't do it around me."

I sighed. All drugs were dangerous, but LSD was one to be particularly wary of. It could cause nonstop hallucinations, and depending on the dosage, they could be either subtle or severe. If she was hanging about at the lighthouse, if she was ever high whilst she was there, she could have seen what I'd seen, what Ally had seen, she could have opened the door in her mind so wide it had been impossible to shut again.

"The house where Moira lived, is it still there?"

"Aye," Mrs Ludmore said, "it's still there."

"Who lives in it now?"

"No one."

"It's abandoned too?"

"It is. There's no shortage of houses on Skye, or land to build them on. Why live where there's been trouble?"

The people on Skye clearly believed in karma as much as they believed in the blue men. Superstitions and fears ran deep. But it wasn't just here. It was everywhere I'd ever been.

Having finished my tea, I checked my watch. It was nearly three o' clock – the day was already on the wane. We left the Ludmores' shortly afterwards, and they, as Mrs Grant and Mr MacIver had done, agreed that we could come back and talk to their children if it proved necessary, although Mrs Ludmore showed more reticence than the others.

"I wish you the best," she'd said, "in tackling what's out there. I don't doubt for one minute that you're as gifted as you say, I've known one or two similar to you in my time, but…" and here she'd paused. "All that talk of Moira, I'm more worried now than ever. I want to protect Craig, not involve him any more in what's happening."

Mr Ludmore had spoken next, his blue eyes beseeching. "What exactly is happening, do you actually have any idea? Because I'll tell you something, I'm flummoxed. Is it a ghost? One of those who was shipwrecked, or all of them perhaps?"

"I don't know what it is," I answered, standing on their doorstep, shivering with the cold. "But one thing I want you to know is I'm doing my best to find out."

Mrs Ludmore shuffled slightly. "It must be hard, having the sight. I wouldn't want it."

"I don't have any choice," was my reply.

"Aye, I don't suppose you do."

Finally on our way again, I checked my watch a second time.

"What's worrying you?" Angus said, as we sat in the car, the heater turned up high.

"The light and how it's fading."

"It is. It'll be full dark soon."

"I'm wondering what to do next, find McCarron, go to the graveyard, or visit Moira's house."

"Moira's house?" he visibly jolted at that. "Why?"

"Because the Camerons disappearance and her suicide might be linked."

"I don't see how."

"Nor do I, but there's only one way to find out."

"Moira's dead," he muttered.

"And guess who can speak with the dead? Come on, then. Moira's house it is."

Chapter Twelve

THE further we drove, the harder it rained – battering the windscreen and the side windows, as if livid at what we were doing: stirring things up further.

"So come on," Angus said, squinting as he drove. "What's your theory regarding Moira?"

I angled my head to look at him. "Angus, you seem slightly het up about my decision to go to Moira's house. Were you fond of her by any chance?"

"I told you, she was bonny."

"You fancied her, you mean."

Briefly he looked at me, his cheeks matching his hair. "You're incredibly blunt, do you know that?"

"And you're transparent."

"That's as maybe."

I tried unsuccessfully to suppress a smile. "So it's true, you did?"

He snorted. "I don't know what red-blooded Scotsman wouldn't."

"Redheaded *and* red-blooded? An explosive combination," I remarked.

He smiled too this time. "Aye, well, maybe you'll find out one day."

"Let's focus on Moira, shall we? Do you have a picture

of her?"

He shook his head. "No, more's the pity. I'd have liked a picture, but it doesn't matter, not really, I remember her as though I can see her still." Once again he described her hair, her eyes, the angel that she was, in his eyes as well as in her parents'.

"But she had a wild streak?"

"She was fun," he insisted. "Old people often confuse the two."

"Drugs aren't necessarily fun." I might sound like a maiden aunt rather than a young woman, but drugs were taking it one step too far, especially in the circumstances.

"The drugs may have had nothing to do with her suicide," he replied, just as insistent. "If that's what it was."

"What do you mean?"

"It could have been an accident. She could have gone walking too close to the edge, the cliffs round here give way sometimes, and crumble. It's so hard to believe she'd kill herself; she was always so full of life. It wasn't just me who adored her, everyone did."

"Did you see her towards the end, when she'd supposedly changed?"

"No." With that he emitted a heavy sigh. "Tell me, how does anyone get that low?"

"They just do," I replied, as he brought the car to a stop. Switching off the engine, he sat where he was, staring blindly ahead. "Are you okay?" I asked.

"I'm fine. We're here. This is it."

"Really?" I said, squinting as he'd done earlier.

"You can barely see her house in this weather, but it's there, a few yards away."

Back on the coast, the weather was as wild as it had been

the previous night – another storm riding in angrily on the shoulders of the last one. The thought of getting out of the car and exploring didn't exactly appeal, but if I waited for the weather to clear, I might be waiting until springtime. He seemed to read my mind.

"It's now or never," he said. "This is settling in for the night."

"I don't know how you stand it really, such awful weather, such a lot of the time."

A smile dissolved all worry from his face. "You stand it because when the sun does shine, there's no better place on earth to be. The big sky, the mountains that surround you, the sheer space that's here, and even weather like this. It's an extension of the landscape. It's magical and alive. Aye, that's what draws you back, what keeps you here – some of us anyway – the magic of it all."

"The magic?" I repeated, feeling even colder than I had before.

"That's right," he continued, oblivious to my sudden change of tone, "it gets in your blood. You become a part of it; it becomes a part of you. Man and his surrounds meld."

"I need to get out. I need to breathe."

"Ness?"

I was being serious – I did need to breathe. Fresh air, cold air, I wanted to stand in the rain, and get soaked to the skin. Outside, where just a minute or two ago I'd baulked at being, suddenly felt wonderful. Breathing deeply, I tilted my head and let the rain plaster my hair to my face, let it wash over me. I understood what he was saying about magic, but there was good magic and there was bad magic, white and black. In such a beautiful place, something ugly had reared its head. And it wasn't to do with the spirit world. Suddenly I understood that. There was no point in going to Kilchoan Cemetery to stand over a slab of stone. The ghosts of those who'd been shipwrecked weren't responsible for this, perhaps not even forlorn Moira. What was responsible was something infinitely darker. Despite that, our trip to the deceased girl's house hadn't been in vain. Even if Moira's spirit had flown – and I sincerely hoped it had – the emotions she'd experienced just before she'd fallen to her death, *whilst* she'd fallen, were certain to have left behind a residue – and that might give me an insight into whether her death had been accidental or intentional. If the latter, she'd have been in agony. *No one* contemplates his or her own demise without being in agony. So what had been the cause of it?

Angus had joined me. "Ness, did I say something—"

"Let's go."

"Where?"

"To the house and then the cliff tops."

"The cliff tops, in this weather? Are you mad?"

I ignored his warning and started to walk, having to fight the wind that wanted so desperately to spin me round and send me the other way. There were no other houses nearby; Moira's stood quite alone. Once again, it was the perfect breeding ground. At the house I peered through the broken window into a dark and abandoned interior. A haven for spiders and other wildlife perhaps, but all furniture, all personal belongings, gone.

"Can you get the door open?" Like last night I had to shout to be heard.

"That'll be breaking and entering!" Angus declared.

"I need to get in there."

"Shit. Well… okay."

Although reluctant he obliged, heaving his shoulder against it. *Come on, come on,* I silently urged. Thankfully, it didn't take long to give way. Standing aside, he let me enter first and then followed, shaking the rain from him as a dog might, sending droplets flying.

"I hope this is going to be worth it," he continued in a peevish manner.

"Angus," I explained, "this is a puzzle. My job is to fit all the pieces together, to solve it."

"It's your mission, you mean."

"Don't split hairs, it's the same thing. Just let me tune in."

His eyes widened. "You really think Moira might still be here?"

"What might be left is a trace of her emotions, her thoughts and her feelings. They're energy too and energy takes time to dissipate."

"It's been nearly eight years!"

"A long time, I agree. And yet, in some respects, it's no time at all. Angus, please, I need to concentrate."

Still sullen, he fell silent. Immediately, I closed my eyes, breathed deeply and imagined the light, and the protection it would give me.

Moira, are you here? You don't know me, but I know of you – what a lovely, young, spirited girl you were in life and that towards the end of that life you were troubled. What was it that upset you? Was it enough for you to take your own life? I'm here to help, Moira, not just you, but also others on the island who are living still, and who may be suffering as you once did. If you're here, come forward and let me know.

As I've said, I wanted Moira to have passed, I'd be glad

if she'd escaped her torment, but I was also desperate for some answers. The cottage, however, was benign enough, even in the failing light, no residue tinged with darkness, not downstairs at least. And not upstairs either, I discovered, although in her bedroom my emotional state became somewhat altered: I felt sad, tearful, bewildered and angry, emotions I was familiar with, but which this time weren't mine.

Did you see something at the lighthouse, Moira? Visions.

And if she had, had they driven her out of her house, to the cliff tops, over the grassy edge and into the sea below – where the storm kelpies were waiting oh so patiently?

I turned to Angus. "Show me where she died."

"I'll take you as close as I dare, but please, listen to me when I say to go no further."

I nodded in agreement. I knew about spiritual perils, he knew about the perils of his home turf – I respected that.

Leaving the cottage behind, Angus securing the door as best he could, we battled our way forwards yet again, heads down, hands in pockets, struggling but determined – at least I was. I could feel it. The closer I got to the cliff's edge, the more intense it became – a battle of another kind: Moira's against whatever it was that had launched an attack. Because that's what it had done, as it had with me and with Ally too. As I'd suspected, she'd opened the door in her mind a little too wide. Her dabbling with LSD had left her vulnerable and this thing liked vulnerable, it *fed* on vulnerable.

Another vision came to mind – Moira rushing as we were rushing. She was alongside us, a pale image, her shoulders hunched as ours were hunched, her sobs choking her.

Oh, Moira!

I wanted to reach out and hug this tortured young woman, but she was no more than a wisp, a mere memory caught on the breeze.

I'm so sorry for what happened to you.

Tears stung my eyes just as the rain did.

"This is as far as it's safe to go." Angus's voice startled me. For a moment I'd forgotten he was there. "Unless that is, you want to end up like Moira."

I shook my head. "I don't."

Standing still, I forced myself to watch what transpired next, heard the words she was screaming in her head. *No! No! No! I won't do it, I won't. You can't make me. You can't.*

Do what?

"Moira!" I yelled, but it wasn't her, it was a shade rushing ever onwards, no stopping, no stumbling, with no hesitation at all.

Angus grabbed me by the shoulders, his expression pained too. "Is she here? Is Moira still here?"

"No, Angus, she's gone. Just be thankful she has."

Chapter Thirteen…

Chapter Fourteen

WAS death the only way to stop these attacks? If so, Ally and her parents were in more danger than I thought, with that danger increasing by the day. Back at Angus's house, both the night and the storm were in full bloom as we gathered round the dining table, Eilidh serving dinner, whilst I discussed with them the significance of the number thirteen.

"I think it stems back to the last supper," Eilidh said, ladling a generous serving of macaroni cheese onto my plate. "There's some honeyed neeps to go with it too. Dig in."

"Do you mean Jesus and his disciples?" asked Angus, also digging in. "Twelve disciples plus Jesus sitting down to eat for the last time, equals unlucky."

Eilidh took her seat too. "Well, it was, wasn't it? Judas was the thirteenth member of the party to arrive and because of him Jesus was crucified."

We both nodded, unable to argue with that.

"But actually, the number thirteen is significant throughout the Bible," she stated. "I can't remember everything I've ever heard, who can? But, Angus, I discussed this very topic with your father once, way before the game started at the lighthouse." Having finished a mouthful of food, she looked at me. "Kenneth was very knowledgeable, he used to spend a lot of time reading. I think it's lovely when a man reads. I wish our son took after him a bit more in that respect."

"Och," Angus dismissed. "I read enough."

"You do not, and that's a fact," retorted Eilidh, but it was a good-natured jibe. "According to Kenneth, there were thirteen famines in the bible, and in one of the gospels, Jesus mentions thirteen things that defile a person, the evil eye being one of them! Can you imagine? What else did he say? Erm... something about the Book of Revelation, that its thirteenth chapter is reserved for Satan." She shrugged, nonchalantly I thought considering the subject. "So you see, just like 666, thirteen has its connotations."

She was right and it was in that very chapter that God had indeed numbered the beast 666. In contrast, seven was the number of perfection, re-emphasising the former as something flawed or incomplete – to the power of three.

"Then there's King Arthur," Eilidh informed us. "He fought twelve battles successfully, but during the thirteenth was mortally wounded. As for Merlin, he spent years searching for the Thirteen Treasures of Britain. Meant to be wielded by the righteous and the brave, woe betide they should fall into the wrong hands, which of course they did.'

As she spoke, my frustration grew. Numerology was a vast and complex subject, it'd take years of study to understand more than the basics.

"Have you got a library on Skye?" I asked, wondering if I could at least get started.

"A mobile one," answered Eilidh, "it's not due for a couple more weeks though."

Silently I cursed. The basics would have to do.

"You know I've heard tell," Eilidh had got the bit between the teeth, "that in some hotels there's no thirteenth floor, not officially anyway, they go straight from twelve to fourteen. Silly if you ask me, if it's there, what's the point in pretending?" She sipped some water. "Also, some streets don't have a number thirteen either. As for Friday the thirteenth…"

"Of course!" I reply. "Friday the thirteenth, they've even made slasher films about it, reinforcing the taboo."

"Have you seen those films, Ness?" Angus asked. "They're pretty good."

"No, I haven't. They really don't appeal."

"Michael Myers a bit much for you, is he?"

"Get your films right, Angus. Michael Myers was in *Halloween*."

"Oh damn, was he?"

"He is, but then… Halloween falls on the 31st October. That's thirteen backwards."

"So it is," Angus said, almost in wonder. "I'd never considered that. And in a witches' coven, there's always thirteen, isn't there?" The expression on my face clearly gave him cause for concern. "It's a rhetorical question," he added. "I'm not asking *you* specifically." Before I could smile to show I'd been joking, he rushed on. "I'll tell you something else, something I learnt in school. You think there are twelve signs of the zodiac, don't you?"

I was confused. "That's because there are."

"Aye, but there are *thirteen* constellations. One got ditched – Ophiuchus – because when the Babylonians invented the calendar over three thousand years ago, they based it on twelve months only. Perhaps they were suspicious about the number thirteen too?"

I shook my head, also in wonder: I hadn't been taught anything that cool in school.

"'I worked out once upon a time," Angus continued, "that if we had thirteen months as the zodiac suggests, we'd end up with a perfect twenty-eight day month, every month. Mind you, having a birthday in the thirteenth month, I'm not actually sure I'd fancy it."

Lucky for some, it was unlucky for others – myself included once upon a time.

We'd finished eating, but Eilidh still looked thoughtful. I gazed at her curiously, trying to catch what was on her mind. Sometimes I could do that, read thoughts, but it was a developing skill, and one I hadn't quite got to grips with yet. I took the easy route, and asked her outright instead. "Eilidh, has something else occurred to you?"

"Aye, something that Kenneth and I mused upon if you like, when we first found out the kids were playing that game at the lighthouse. He was very protective was Kenneth, Angus is our only son and we waited a long time for him." At this she smiled indulgently, which he, like only the very loved can, rolled his eyes at. "He never liked them doing it," she confided, "used to get agitated, whereas I said it was just a bit of harmless fun. More fool me. I'm not sure who liked to think they invented the game, do you, Angus?"

"No idea. It was just something that... came into being."

"Well, whoever it was, maybe they knew about One Hundred Ghost Stories, which is a centuries old Japanese tradition."

"One hundred ghost stories?" Angus spluttered. "That'd take forever! Thirteen was sometimes bad enough,

102

especially whenever Maire MacTavish was involved. I've told you about her, haven't I, Ness, the romance writer, the one that went on and on?"

"Yes, you have," I answered, before turning to Eilidh. "What's this tradition? I'd love to hear about it."

"A group of people sit in a circle, up to one hundred in number, a candle placed before them. It's not a game, but a ritual. I can't remember the Japanese name for it, but Kenneth would. They'd tell a story, blow out the candle, counting all the way to one hundred. Once it's done, and they're in complete darkness, a ghost is supposed to appear in the middle of the circle. See? It's just the same really. The same principle anyway."

"Know any horror stories attached to that particular practice?" Angus asked his mother.

"No, laddie, of course I don't. Why would I? I just know of it, that's all, thanks to your very well read dad. What I was wondering is, if whoever started the game at the lighthouse knew of the ritual, if it was their inspiration?"

Whether they did or not maybe didn't matter. What mattered was that the game had history, and more than that, an *expectation* attached – one that was supernatural. As I've said before, some games shouldn't be played; they should be left well alone.

I came to a decision. "Eilidh, once Angus and I have cleared the dishes, would you mind if we went out again?"

It was Angus who replied. "Where are we going, back to the lighthouse?"

"No. When we go there again, it'll be in daylight. I want to speak to Liam's father and from what you've told me about him, I'm guessing where he'll be."

"At the pub."

I winked cheekily at him. "If you drive me I'll buy you a lemonade."

* * *

Waiting in the hallway for Angus, who'd quickly visited the bathroom, Eilidh came to stand beside me. "You put a spring in his step, so you do."

"Who? Angus?"

"Aye, and little wonder, you're a bonny lass."

Embarrassed, I lifted one hand to push at my hair. "Thank you, but I'm really not."

My protestation surprised her. "Why are you so quick to disagree? Surely your mother's told you countless times how bonny you are?"

"My mother?" I almost choked on the words. "Sorry, I'm so sorry," I said, realising how bad that must have looked. "Erm… no, she didn't actually, not often." Not *ever* more like.

Reaching out, Eilidh took my arm. "Then more fool her. She *should* have told you."

A brief moment of silence hung between us, during which I attempted to change the subject. "I hope the pub isn't too far."

It didn't work.

"I'm glad you came to Skye," she continued, "and I'm grateful for your help. We need it. Like you, I don't think the situation's going to get any better or go away on its own." I looked at her, stunned. At no point had I shared that point of view with her, and yet still she'd picked up on it. "The thing is, Ness, you have to believe in yourself.

You're a special person. You're kind, you're beautiful and you're talented. But if you don't think you are, if you keep denying it, then what good is any of it? Whatever we're facing, you're its equal. I believe in you and I'll help too, in any way I can. There are a lot of us that will, we won't question what you do. You're not something outlandish here, you're a hero."

There was no way I could answer, not when a sob had lodged in my throat. Thankfully I didn't have to. Angus appeared, all brisk efficiency, rubbing his hands together as though in excited anticipation before shooing me out the door. It took the entire twenty-minute car journey for me to regain composure after what Eilidh had said, my head turned from Angus all the while, as I stared into the stormy darkness, seeing nothing but my own pitiful reflection staring back. It was so white against the night, so small and insignificant. A hero she'd called me, riding up here on a plane instead of a charger, ready to tackle what had been causing trouble. Was I such? No. A hero wouldn't have done as I'd done in the past.

"Here we are, at the oldest pub on Skye."

I shook my head in surprise. "Already?"

"We are indeed. Were you asleep by the way, you were awful quiet."

"I... erm... might have dozed off for a minute or two," I lied, having to lean forward so that I could see the white-washed building we were slowly passing, one that ran the length of several houses. On it were words picked out in black: The Stein Inn. "How old is it?" I asked.

"Dates back to 1790 according to a plaque at the entrance. Supposed to be haunted too, be interesting to see if you think so."

"I hope not. There's no time to get side-tracked."

"Aye, well, the only spirits I've ever seen in there are from the local distillery."

As we hurried back towards the pub from the car park, the rain having eased slightly, though the wind was still fierce, Angus told me there was a loch to our left. I looked over, but I have to say, I'd never have guessed, the clouds once again having erected a wall.

We reached the porch and stopped to catch our breaths.

"It's beautiful here on a summer's day," he continued when he was able. "The loch's as still as anything."

"Being the oldest pub on Skye, it must get besieged with tourists."

"Tourists? I should think most of them opt for far sunnier climes than this. No, it's peaceful on the whole, one of my favourite locations. Sitting with a pint, staring out over the water, there's a healing quality to it. You should try it sometime."

Anger flared. "Sorry? What do you mean by that?"

"What? Nothing, I…"

"First your mother and now you."

"My mother…?"

"There's nothing wrong with me!"

"I'm sorry, I really don't—"

"I don't need your pity. I don't want it!"

"Ness, will you calm down, I was just saying, that's all."

"But that whole healing thing…"

"Aye, it is, it's exactly that, it's special. But I wasn't implying *you* needed healing."

"It's just…" Again, my voice trailed off.

"Although to be honest, doesn't everyone, to some degree or other? Life can deliver some hard knocks."

I lowered my head – all fight gone. "Life is what it is, it's a learning curve."

He leant a little closer to me – as close as he dared I suppose. "Ness, what's happening here, if it's putting you under too much pressure—"

"It's not, I'm trying to understand it, that's all."

"Everyone affected is. You're not alone."

Then how come I felt it, especially at this moment, standing in the wind-blown porch of an ancient pub in one of the United Kingdom's most far-flung places? How come I felt more alone than ever? I blinked heavily. "I'm tired, I think. It's been another long day."

"It has. Are you sure you want to go in, or shall we just go home and get some rest?"

"We're here now."

"Come on, then, let's get it over and done with. If he's here, I don't know what state he's going to be in. Sometimes he has to be carried back to his bed."

"We'll soon find out, I guess."

Entering the pub, a welcome blast of heat hit us courtesy of a fire that was devouring logs a few feet away. Also in close proximity was a man sitting on a stool at the bar; he had very red cheeks, a mop of white hair and a stomach to rival that of Father Christmas.

"Ron, how are you?" Angus greeted. "This is Ness, a friend of mine. Ness, this is Ron."

Ron's eyes were already glazed with a somewhat rheumy quality to them, his nose large and rounded, reminded me of a chunk of cheese. One hand gripped his pint, as though hanging on to it for dear life, the other he extended towards me. I noticed it was shaking slightly. "Pleased to meet you. It's a wild night you've come out on."

"Needs must," answered Angus. "Now, Ness, what are you having?"

"Erm… coke will be fine."

"Nothing harder?"

"No thanks." Seeing how the hard stuff affected Ron had had an off-putting effect.

"No problem," he replied amiably, "and I guess it's a lemonade for me."

I tore my gaze away briefly from Ron to smile at him.

"So," Ron continued. "You're English."

"For my sins, yes."

"My lad's just gone over the border to Carlisle, he's working in a boatyard there."

"Liam?"

Ron looked astonished. "Aye. You know him, do you?"

Angus answered before I could, handing me my drink at the same time. "No, she doesn't, but Liam's who we've come to talk to you about."

Ron's whole demeanour changed, he sat further upright, suspicion sharpening his gaze. "And why is that, may I ask?"

"Erm…" I stuttered. For the second time, I wished Angus wouldn't just steam in like that, that he'd take things a bit slower. Next thing he'd be telling Ron I was a psychic.

"She's a psychic you see, investigating what happened at the lighthouse, like a detective almost. In fact, she works for the police too, and the council, don't you, Ness?"

I could have kicked him – right there and then in that genteel pub that was thankfully empty, apart from Ron and a barmaid who had since disappeared.

"Angus—" I began, intending to have another go at him, but Ron cut me off.

"Liam's stint at the lighthouse, it's over and done with. He's moved on."

Before I could reply, he reached for his glass and drank from it, several long draughts that rendered it dry. I couldn't help but be impressed and Angus too by the looks of him.

Belching, he then yelled for the barmaid. "Jan, where are you? Get me another."

Jan appeared – world-weary Jan; a Jan who looked far from impressed with Ron's behaviour, who'd seen it all before, many times no doubt.

"We're going to call it a night soon," she warned, taking his glass from him and duly refilling it. "No one's coming out, not in this weather, no one in their right mind any-way." Glancing at us, she shrugged as if she couldn't care less if her words caused offence. Handing him his glass, she added, "You've ten minutes, fifteen at the most."

Whilst she did another disappearing act, Ron drank again, but managed to stop about a third of the way through this time.

"Look," I said, having waited patiently, "Angus's uncle wanted me to come here, after... well, after what happened with Ally Dunn. I presume you know about that?"

"Aye I do, I keep my ear to the ground. But what's it got to do with Liam?"

"I'm wondering if what happened with Ally is linked in any way with the Camerons' sudden disappearance."

"Something supernatural, you mean?" Yet again his hand gripped his pint, but he didn't raise it to his lips, he continued staring at me.

I swallowed. "Yes. Exactly that."

"You know about the girl who threw herself off the

cliffs?"

I heard Angus breathe inwards, but I simply nodded. "Moira? Yes I do."

"Think it's linked with her too, do you?"

"It could be."

Silence descended, not companionable, it felt explosive. Was Ron going to start yelling at me to get out of his favourite watering hole, and take my witchy ways with me? I always half-expected that reaction. He did no such thing. When he started speaking again, his voice was low, ominous even.

"They weren't right, the Camerons. They came from an island more remote than this one. Barra, do you know it? Less than a thousand people live there. Island people – *remote* island people – I'm wary of them sometimes. The Camerons came to man that lighthouse and largely they kept themselves to themselves. Even home schooled their young 'uns, well Mrs Cameron did, didn't want them mixing, picking up funny ways." He bellowed with laughter at that, causing a dog to howl, one I hadn't noticed before, lounging behind the other side of the bar – Jan's dog, it must be. "Ironic, isn't it, that they should be the ones worried about funny ways."

I didn't know whether his prejudice was widespread or peculiar to him, but I listened carefully nonetheless, desperate for more clues.

"Liam never liked working there, truth be told, much less living in that cabin. It's a bleak place, awful. *Da,* he said, *it's like living at the end of the world.* I sympathised, I did, but a job's a job and on Skye, you cannae afford to be fussy. He grew fond of the kids well enough, Caitir and Niall, playing games with them when their parents were out of earshot, having a bit of a laugh. Ach, Liam was just a big kid himself in many ways. Once the parents found out though, they put to a stop to it, told him to do his job and nothing more, that he wasn't to 'interfere'. He was there a year before Cameron insisted he wasn't needed anymore. He had to pack his bags and go. Liam was glad of it though. He said that during the last few months they'd grown even stranger, the kids too, although to be fair, he hadn't seen the youngsters in a while, they barely ever roamed the hillsides, were always kept inside. Terrible that is, to keep kids inside, they need fresh air to fill their lungs, to make them proper Highlanders. I went to pick Liam up and sought out Cameron, if only to shake his hand, to thank him for giving my lad a job in the first place, no hard feelings, like. Despite everything, the job would look good on his CV; it'd help him to go on to better things. So I went looking for him, as I said, and found him at the top of the tower, just staring at the sea. Big man he was, built like a brick shithouse. I said my piece, I thanked him and he ignored me. Can you believe it? He stood there, as still as a statue, with his back to me, as if in a trance. I went back down, passed the house on my way to the car, and noticed for the first time that the curtains were closed, despite it being such a bonny day. I no longer wanted to thank him, I can tell you. I just wanted to get away. I had a sense – a *strong* sense – that we'd made a lucky escape; that Liam had got out in the nick of time. I felt guilty too, that he'd even been there in the first place. A job's a job, I'd said that, but that place, on that day…" He shook his head. "No one's ever that desperate. Soon after that the Camerons upped and left, and good riddance to them."

Having delivered this spiel, he at last finished the other

half of his pint. As soon as that glass was empty, Jan reappeared, a troubled look on her face. Had she been listening to Ron, I wondered?

"Come on," she said, "away with you all. I've had enough."

We quickly finished our drinks as Ron eased himself off his stool. As we made our way to the door, he staggered a little and I reached out a hand to steady him.

"So you're a psychic, are you?"

"I… I have a sixth sense, yes."

"A miracle worker too?"

I frowned. "A miracle worker? No. I'm just trying to help."

"I don't want you to contact Liam, I want him left alone. He's happy now, he's settled, out of harm's way."

I stood my ground. "What about those who remain in harm's way? What about Ally?"

"Stupid kids shouldn't have gone to the lighthouse in the first place."

"But they did."

He looked at me for a moment and then relented. "Aye, they did."

Angus held the door open and we stood in the porch once more, whilst Jan slid the bolts home on the other side, making a point. Ron stood swaying in between us. "I see things sometimes," he said, his manner conspiratorial. "When I've had one too many, but that doesn't mean to say they're not there. The drink, it does something."

"It opens you up," I said, thinking about Moira and the LSD.

He nodded. "Aye, that it does. Please, lass, I'm asking you, don't get Liam involved. He's a good lad, a conscientious lad. If you contact him, he'll come back, won't even think twice about it. He's like you, not psychic, I don't mean that, but he likes to help."

"We can't get in touch if you don't give us his details," I reminded him.

"Well, I'm not going to, not right now."

"Fair enough," I said, disappointed in his decision.

Staring wistfully outwards, he staggered again. This time Angus caught him. "Will I give you a lift home, Ron?" he asked.

"Away with you!" Ron waved a hand at him. "I can walk. The fresh air will do me good."

Although not convinced, Angus didn't object. "We'd best away ourselves then."

All three of us started walking, Ron veering off to the right. As I watched him go, I considered what we'd learnt – something – but not enough. I was still confused. If only we could speak to Liam, it would help further, but we also had to respect his father's wishes.

Heads down again, slightly despondent, we marched onwards. Because of my stance, I didn't realise Ron was making his way back towards us until Angus nudged me.

Coming to a standstill in front of us, it was me the old man focused on. "I've no wish to put you in harm's way. Look at you, you're no more than a wee slip of a girl."

"I'm stronger than I look."

"It might be nothing…"

"Ron, please. If Moira is connected to this, there's already been one death that we know about. Ally Dunn… I'm concerned for her too. Do I…" I hesitated. "Do I need to go to Barra? Perhaps the Camerons have gone back there?"

"Barra?" He spat the word at me. "You'll not get to Barra in this weather. You'll not get there 'til the springtime."

"Damn!" I said under my breath. Could this case wait that long? I honestly didn't think so. "Angus?" I questioned.

"He's right. There's no way. Not in this."

Ron noticed how stricken I looked. "Don't take on, lass, it's not there you need to go anyway."

"Oh? Where then?" I asked, doubly confused.

"It's your namesake, Loch Ness. On the banks, overlooking the waters, there's a house, Balskeyne. One with a reputation."

"What kind of reputation?"

"A bad one." As he said it, a gust of wind blew him backwards. Quickly he fought against it and straightened up. "Liam heard Cameron talk about Balskeyne once, to his wife. And in the last few months he was at Minch, there used to come a visitor there, when none had been before. It was a man Liam didn't like the look of; he told me there was something about him... something *unclean*. That's when the Camerons changed, when this man started up his visits. Never friendly, they went to being downright odd."

"Balskeyne?" I turned to Angus. "Have you heard of this house?"

"Oh, aye, I've heard of it. But under the circumstances, Ness, I wish to God I hadn't."

Chapter Fifteen

"WE can't do it, we can't go there. I'd rather take my chances with going to Barra."

"Why can't we go there? What's wrong with it, tell me."

Ron had finally left us and we were in Angus's car again, just sitting there, in an empty car park, the wind and the rain as relentless as ever.

"It's just… It can't have anything to do with the lighthouse, it can't have."

"Angus! Will you just tell me what you know?"

"It's… Well… It all goes back to the sixties; a man came to live there – Isaac Leonard." He laughed. "Harmless enough name, isn't it, but apparently he was far from that."

"What was he?"

"I'll tell you what he was rumoured to be: a Black Magician. Have you not heard of him, Ness?"

"I've heard of a few, but not him, no." Inside, my gut was churning. Magic of a warped kind was exactly what I'd feared.

"He bought the house for the purpose of a ritual he wanted to carry out there, one he'd studied in an ancient text apparently, dating back to the Middle Ages. There was a list of rules in preparation for this ritual. You had to abstain from alcohol, remain celibate, and meditate – a lot.

The house itself played a role too. It had to be in a secluded location, more or less, with a door opening to the west, in front of which was a gravel or sand path. At the end of this path, there needed to be a lodge of some sort. That's supposed to be where the spirits congregate. The purpose of it all was—"

"To invoke your Guardian Angel," I finished.

"So you *have* heard of Leonard?"

"Just the ritual, it's one that several, perhaps more notable, Black Magicians have followed, I'm not sure how successfully. It's from *The Book of Abramelin*, which, as you say, is a medieval grimoire, one that surged in popularity during this century and the last. I'm no expert regarding it, but yes, I've heard of that at least. This Guardian Angel, as they call it, was supposed to impart magical wisdom, which the recipient could then use for good or bad purposes. The trouble is, it's usually the latter, being as this sort of thing appeals to the megalomaniacs amongst us."

"Megalomaniacs? So, you've never been tempted then?"

"Angus! I may be many things, but hopefully not that!"

He grinned. "No, I have to admit, you don't strike me as such."

"Good," I answered, just as he sighed. All joking aside, I reached out. "You okay?" He was concerned earlier that this task might be having an effect on me, but what about him?

"I'm fine," he assured me. "It's odd, that's all, sitting in a pub car park, late at night, talking about Black Magic of all things."

I agreed. "It is odd, but we're doing it for a reason."

"Aye, I know… to help."

"Unless, it's too much—"

"It's not. Not with you by my side."

I smiled. Like his mother; he had such faith in me. "So, Leonard carried out this ritual at this house on the banks of Loch Ness. What's the consensus? Did he succeed?"

"He may have done, certainly that's what people around here like to think."

"But no one knows for sure."

"They know it's got a bad atmosphere. *I* know it's got a bad atmosphere."

"You?" I was confused and then the penny dropped. "Ah, I see, it was another place you went to as a kid, looking for thrills."

He shrugged. "I've told you, there's not much to do around here."

"Except get involved in a bit of Satanism."

"Aye, well it's something, isn't it?"

I looked at him, he looked at me, and together we burst out laughing. It felt good, so good. I hadn't laughed like that in… well, I couldn't remember the last time.

"Honestly though," he continued, wiping at his eyes, "it's some place, a big old manor house, owned by a rock star after Leonard, although we'd no idea who it was back then."

"Do you know now?"

"Oh aye, it was Robbie Nelson from the band, The Ridge. He was interested in its history, you see, all that occult stuff. The thing is, he never stayed there, not really. An interest is one thing, but the chance to experience it, or at least the aftermath of it, I suppose that's quite another."

"So what year was it when you went there?"

"It must have been around '75, perhaps early in '76, I was twelve, nearly thirteen."

"Wow, that young?"

"Aye, I was the youngest that night, by a fair bit actually."

"I'm surprised your parents let you."

"They never knew," Angus confessed. "As far as they were concerned I was at a sleepover at one of the other lads' houses."

"Ah, I see, that old chestnut."

"It came in handy a fair few times."

"So it was well before Moira?"

"Oh aye, it was before she… you know. Anyway, Nelson had moved out by then, and it was empty for a while. Whoa!" He ran his hands through his hair as he began his troubled journey down memory lane. "It's not as if we went inside the house or anything, we didn't want to break in, get into trouble with the law, but the grounds and the lodge at the bottom of the garden, were bad enough. There were five of us: three lads and two lasses, and as I say I was the youngest of the lot, Will, was the eldest at eighteen. I'm telling you, all of us had goose bumps the minute we set foot on that land. The only way I can describe it is, it was like a thousand eyes were watching us, hiding in the trees that surrounded the place, eyes that didn't belong to anything of this world; they belonged to monsters instead. And that's not my youth and immaturity talking – we *all* felt that way, even Will. We tried to nudge each other on, you know, be brave, but when we got to the house and started peering in through the windows, one of the girls – Lottie – started to scream blue murder. She thought she saw a figure in there, one that was impossibly tall, blacker than black, and who was glaring at her. It was the eyes that did it; they were glowing, she said, neon yellow or something. As she stared, transfixed, the figure lifted its hand to point."

"What happened then?" I asked, able to vividly imagine it all.

"We ran, as fast as our legs could take us. We got out of there. Will had his dad's car, so we piled into that and drove back to the Kyle of Lochalsh. We slept all night in his car, well, what few hours were left, and then we caught the first ferry the next morning. A cousin of mine ran the ferry at the time, so it's not as if we had to pay. But I'll tell you, none of us returned, not as far as I know."

"It could all have been imagination though, preconceptions kicking in?"

He denied it. "Something was wrong there, very wrong."

Perhaps. Just as something was wrong here.

I thought about what I'd learnt. "So, Leonard was at Balskeyne in the sixties, but by the early seventies it belonged to a rock star?"

"Aye, and later on, in '76, it was turned into a guesthouse. Can you credit it? I mean, really? Who'd want to stay there knowing who it had once belonged to?"

"But that's the thing, people don't *always* know. Do you research the history of every house or hotel you've ever stayed at?"

"I've only ever stayed at a handful," he admitted.

"Even so, have you?"

"No, of course not."

"There you go then."

"Yeah, but when it's got a notorious history?"

"I've never heard of Isaac Leonard or Balskeyne. There'd be many who haven't or, if they have, who'd dismiss it as nonsense. Is the house still being run as a guesthouse?"

"Och, I've no idea. There are two roads that skirt Loch Ness, the main road and the back road – Balskeyne's on the banks of the back road. I never tend to go that way, it's too, you know… twisty turny."

"Twisty turny? That's a novel way of putting it."

"But you get my meaning?"

"Aye, I do."

He raised an eyebrow at my impression of him, seemed to find it amusing enough.

"What I don't get," I continued, "is the timing. It's all off."

"How'd you mean?"

"Leonard lived at Balskeyne in the sixties, but by the seventies, the time that the Camerons moved into the lighthouse, a rock star had bought it, one who hardly ever stayed there apparently, and after he sold it, it was turned into a guesthouse. So how's it all connected, *if* it is connected? Do you know what happened to Isaac Leonard?"

"What happened to him and whether he's still alive or dead, I don't know."

"It's something we need to find out."

He cocked his head to the side. "Oh, and how do you propose we do that?"

"You can take me there tomorrow and we can ask whoever's living there now."

"Do I get another lemonade for my efforts?"

"If you let me drive I'll make it a wee dram instead."

"Ness Patterson, you've just got yourself a deal."

Feeling perhaps lighter-hearted than we should, we made our way back home.

* * *

120

Ness, you're dreaming again.

It was little solace. Not when the dream was this bad.

I'm at my desk, writing, as one of the teenagers had written, scribing the number thirteen, over and over.

Why thirteen?

Because it's a powerful number or at least that's what people think. Certainly it has a hold on me. I can't stop myself, the paper beneath my marker beginning to tear with the pressure I'm exerting. When it runs out, I start on the walls, determined to fill every inch.

What does it mean? What does it all mean?

There's someone in the room with me, laughing. Who could it be? Angus?

I shake my head. No. He doesn't laugh like that. His is a sweet laugh.

You like him don't you, Ness?

No... yes... not in that way... as a friend.

You want him?

It's not me talking to myself anymore, someone else is asking the question.

I swing round, holding the marker as though it were a dagger.

"Who's there?" I can't see whoever's with me. They're hiding in the shadows, but I can feel their gaze, imagine well enough the colour of their eyes – yellow like pus.

I face the wall again. Whatever's in the shadows can stay there. I don't want to know.

13. 13. 13.

It's such a bold number, a number that screams at you.

Just like the figure in the shadows is screaming. No longer laughing, there are words tumbling from its mouth instead, not all of them intelligible. Although some are.

You. Want. No one.

I ignore it.

13. 13. 13.

I'm stabbing at the wall, unable to stop myself, big chunks of masonry tumbling too.

Remember, Ness?

Stabbing, stabbing, stabbing, obliterating what's in front of me; that damned number.

What you did to me?

My hand clenches tight around the marker.

What you did to yourself?

My nails dig into the palm of my hand.

Blood. Why is there always so much blood?

What you did to all of us. When you were thirteen, Ness. When you were thirteen.

Chapter Sixteen

INCREDIBLY the sun was shining the next day, although it was still bitterly cold. After more scrambled eggs on toast – and this time I managed a strip of bacon too – Angus and I journeyed towards Kyleakin, for the short journey across the water to the mainland. The scenery was so breath-taking it took my mind off the restless night I'd had and the dream. Instead of fretting about it, I immersed myself in the might of nature instead, the Cuillin Mountains once more the star of the show, so black against the blue sky, like sentinels standing guard. As I gazed at them, Angus told me about the fairy pools that were hidden amongst them, named for the belief that the fairies, or the little people as they were known hereabouts, bathed in them by starlight.

"And some big people do too," he added.

"Don't tell me, you included."

He laughed. "You're getting to know me very well. Although I've not gone for a dip by starlight, I'm not that daft – the water's freezing enough by day. Another place I'll have to take you, if we have the time, is the fairy glen. Aye, that's worth a trip, if just to admire the strange landscape. It's full of green knolls that tower upwards."

"Where is it?" I asked.

"Up near Uig."

"Uig? Okay, sounds good, I'd love to go." I'd scheduled in a week for this trip and a good portion of that had gone already – another three or four days, that's all I could really spare. Hopefully, that'd be enough. If it was, and if there was time for a little sightseeing as Angus suggested, all well and good. Although I was my own boss to a large extent, I'd said to Angus that I had other projects in the pipeline, plus I missed my flat, my own space. As lovely and as hospitable as Eilidh and Angus were, I needed time to myself. I always had.

The mainland was just as lovely as Skye, so easy to fall in love with. I'd never been to Scotland before and I was amazed at how different it was to where I lived in Lewes, the historic county town of East Sussex. There we were surrounded by gently rolling hills, described by Rudyard Kipling as *'Our blunt, bow-headed, whale-backed Downs'* – beautiful in their own right, but not rugged, not mighty, not like anything I was encountering here.

Angus had driven, despite me offering once again. 'You look tired,' he'd said. 'If we stop for a drink later, maybe you can take over, but otherwise, I'm more than happy to take the wheel.'

He was right; I *was* tired. Even my bones felt heavy. Despite the dazzling views, I yawned. "How far is it to Balskeyne?"

"Not long now, we'll be there within the hour. Nice weather for a visit, don't you think?"

"Yeah, yeah, it is. The weather's wonderful."

"Such a shame we're not heading for the beach. That's another thing that Skye's got, the most amazing beaches. Just north of Dunvegan is a place called Coral Beach, named after the crushed white coral that's there, it makes the sea look really blue."

Immediately, guilt seized me. "I'm sorry to take you away from enjoying whatever free time you have." I bit my lip. "Maybe I should have driven up, it would have been handy to have had my own car. Actually, is there anywhere I can rent one?"

Angus flapped a hand in the air at me. "Och, I'll not hear of it. I like being with you. I find what you do… interesting."

"Thanks. You're fun to be with too."

My words surprised me. I don't normally tend to say stuff like that, but where was the harm in it? He *was* fun. I really ought to loosen up a little.

The journey – and it had been a long one, three hours door to door – at last came to an end. Balskeyne was close to Fort Augustus, as opposed to Inverness, and not visible from the road, due to a bank of trees that stood like custodians.

"Where do we park?" I asked.

"Just here, on the main road. If we tuck ourselves in, it'll be okay."

As we crossed the road, and skirted round to a gravel path that led upwards, the clouds must have covered the sun, for suddenly the day got darker.

Angus noticed it too. "I hope it's not an omen."

So did I. "Are you… erm… nervous about coming here again after so long?"

"A bit," he admitted. "What about you? Are you nervous?"

"I'm trying not to be. I wonder who lives here now."

"I've not a clue, so we'd best be careful, we don't want to be shot for trespassing."

"Shot?" I repeated, somewhat aghast.

"Relax, I'm joking," he replied, but I could tell from his voice he wasn't convincing himself either. My mind started to work overtime.

"I'll say I thought it was still a guesthouse," I suggested, "that I'd stayed here when it was, years ago, as a kid. I could even ask if there's a room available."

"For the both of us?"

"Well… yeah."

"Who shall we say we are," asked Angus. "Mr and Mrs Smith?"

"Mr and Mrs…? Don't push it, Angus."

He laughed. "Sorry, I really wasn't. But your ploy, it might work."

"I hope so. If I can find out anything about the house, it'll be a bonus. I might even be able to tune into something."

"And that'd be a bonus too, do you think?"

I grimaced. "Hmm, maybe not."

We continued up the path, our feet kicking at stones. It had to be secluded for the sake of the ritual, and secluded it was. Where was the house for goodness' sake? Rounding a corner, I held my breath – soon I'd be able to see it, in all its murky glory.

"Bloody hell!" Angus exclaimed.

"Christ!" I added.

There was nothing glorious about what was in front of us; it was a hollow, burnt out wreck.

"What's happened?" I said, at the same time as Angus pointed out the obvious: "There's been a fire!"

Dragging my eyes away, I turned to him. "Didn't you realise?"

126

"I've told you I haven't been here since."

We heard a voice behind us. "Hey there! Who are you? You're on private land."

We turned to see a woman hurrying towards us; she had to be in her late forties or even early fifties, with dark brown hair in a bun, although several strands had escaped, and wearing corduroy trousers and a zip-up fleece. As she drew nearer, I could see fury had caused her complexion to redden, and that she was doing her utmost to contain it.

I held my hands up. "I'm sorry, so sorry. It's just I was here as a kid and—"

"Rubbish! If you'd visited as a child, there's no way you'd come back, not unless you were a stupid child and an even stupider adult. You're another voyeur, wanting to see what all the fuss is about, but there's nothing to see here, not anymore. Please go."

I was stunned, so was Angus. We just stood there, staring at her, as she'd said – stupidly.

Angus recovered first. "You're right, that's a pack of lies. We have come to see what all the fuss is about, but for a good reason, the best of reasons actually. My name is Angus Macbrae and this is Ness Patterson, I'm from Skye, Ness is from Lewes, not the island—"

"I know where Lewes is," she barked.

"Oh, right," Angus dared to speak again. "I can tell from your accent you're not local."

"I'm from London," she said. "West Ken. I live here now though, this is my property."

He inclined his head to the ruin. "But there is no property."

"There's a lodge. I'm comfortable enough in it."

"The lodge," he repeated. "Where the spirits could

gather."

Her fury erupted. "That's it, get off my land. Idiots! Utter idiots! You don't know what you're dealing with. I'm warning you, if you don't go, I'll call the police."

"Please," I said, taking my turn at trying to appease her, "just listen to us, hear us out. It's as my friend says, we've come for the best of reasons, although…" I hesitated, "the worst of reasons too. What happened here, it may be happening again, over on Skye—"

"Don't pretend you know what you're talking about."

"I do though, I honestly do. I'm a psychic."

That surprised her. "A psychic? Prove it."

My heart sank. Prove it? How could I do that? It wasn't as if there was a convenient spirit hovering close by, either good or bad. *You can sometimes catch thoughts.* True, but it wasn't all the time, it was more random than by design. Even so, if I could catch what was on her mind, even just a word or two, it'd be something in our favour.

"If you could formulate a thought," I said, "I'll try and see what it is. I know that's not necessarily proving I'm a psychic, but what it will do is prove I have extra-sensory skills."

"You want me to think something?"

"Besides us being stupid," I added, chancing a smile.

"That would be too easy I suppose." Was that a hint of a smile on her face too?

"Just… pluck something out of the blue," I advised.

"Okay, I will."

She closed her eyes and raised her head a little, as if in salute to the sun.

I was grateful; it allowed me to stare at her unhindered, to focus. What was she thinking? What could she possibly be thinking? I continued to stare, biting at my lip – what the hell was it? Panic set in. Thoughts were easier to detect if the other person was psychic too, or had a degree of psychic ability; with non-psychics it was so much harder. *Oh, please, please, let me get something – a word, two words, a few even.*

If I failed, she was going to run us off her land, and there'd be nothing we could do about it. I doubted severely if my connections with the Sussex police would count for anything – we had to get her permission to look around, we had to. *Come on, please, pick up a word, just a word, anything. Ness, come on!*

Don't try so hard. Those were the words that eventually appeared – all four of them in my mind, perfectly scribed. Was it self-administered advice or could it possibly be…

"Don't try so hard!" I whispered the words in the vain hope I was right.

She opened her eyes and fixed them on me, another slow smile developing. "You know, it really is so much easier if you just allow your gift to flow."

I smiled too, partly in wonder. "You believe me then?"

She nodded.

"And you're psychic too?"

"I'm intuitive. Let's leave it at that. Tell me the truth about why you're here."

As she asked the heavens opened.

"Come on," she said, her back hunched against the sudden downpour, "come to the lodge house. If you're brave enough, that is."

She started running, and without hesitation Angus and I followed her, reaching the door of the tiny structure that stood just a few metres from what remained of Balskeyne.

Disappearing into the bathroom whilst we stood inside the doorway, she returned with towels for us to dry our hair, waiting patiently for us to perform the deed before taking them from us and dropping them back in the bathroom. We were then ushered into a small living room, where a log fire remained unlit and books crowded every surface.

"You like to read?" I said, picking up one book. Not a work of fiction, it was called *Symbols of Eternity*. I quickly scanned the titles of the other books I could see. They were all non-fiction, all dealing with esoteric subjects.

"Take a seat," she said, offering us neither coffee nor tea.

We did, Angus opting for the sofa and having to shift several books aside. I took the armchair that was opposite her, looking longingly at the fire, wishing it were lit.

"What's been happening on Skye?" she said. Regarding bluntness, I'd met my match.

As succinctly as I could I explained, noticing that when I told her about the visions she started to pick at her nails.

"I see," she said, when I'd finished. "So that's the link, the fact that the lighthouse keeper was overheard mentioning Balskeyne."

"And there was the visitor to the lighthouse, someone Liam didn't recognise, someone he didn't like the look of. It was after those visits that Mr Cameron changed."

"It could be something and nothing," she said, leaning into her chair

"But what if it's something?" Angus asked, both of us turning to look at him. "Just saying," he shrugged, going slightly red again.

I returned my gaze to the woman. "Erm… sorry, I don't even know your name…"

"Shelley Cooper-Brown," she replied curtly.

"Shelley, we were… erm… quite shocked to see that the house had burnt down. Did that happen recently?"

"Yes."

"No one was hurt?"

"No one."

I don't know where I got the courage from, but I had to ask. "Did you do it?"

She stared at me for so long that I grew hot and sweaty under her gaze, any chill I'd felt before, forgotten. And then to my relief, she laughed, a deep, throaty sound. We waited patiently until she stopped, until she spoke again.

"I admire your cheek," she said eventually. "In answer to your question, no, I didn't do it. It was an accident, a kitchen fire that got out of hand. I wasn't here you see, I was stocking up on groceries in Inverness. By the time I got back, it was raging. And I let it rage. Everything happens for a reason, and fire can be so wonderfully cleansing."

"Perhaps the lighthouse should go the same way?" I suggested, even more boldly.

"You're an arsonist now as well as a psychic?"

I hung my head. "No. No, I'm not."

"Didn't think so," she said. "There's actually no need to go to such lengths. It's enough if there's an overseer. That's what I am, an overseer, I keep things in check."

"There are plans for the lighthouse to be made into a guesthouse. Angus is going to manage it."

She turned towards him. "You'll be an overseer too."

Angus paled slightly. "I'm not sure I'm up to that," he cried.

"Believe it and you will be," Shelley answered.

"So," I said, "this place, Balskeyne, does it live up to its reputation?"

"Concerning Isaac Leonard? Perhaps. You've told me you know something of the ritual he performed here, one that took many months, much patience, and meticulous planning. He may have been successful to a degree, but that's because he really had chosen the ideal place – this land is drenched in negative energy – long before the house was built."

"Oh?" I said, curious.

"In the twelfth century, there was a kirk here, a church in other words. No one knows for sure why, but one day, during a service, a fire broke out, right at the entrance to the church. There were a lot of people in attendance and none escaped. After that, in the 1760s, Balskeyne was built as a hunting lodge. The owner, Colonel Aleister Fraser, was involved in a duel thereafter and shot dead just feet from his own front door, his blood soaking the land. When Leonard lived here, doing whatever he was doing, a lot of strange goings-on were reported by people hereabouts. There were tales of people dying or mysteriously disappearing, even a butcher who chopped his hand off after receiving a meat order from the house. Part of the ritual involved summoning a number of demons, all harbingers of negative energy; it could have been these who ran amok locally, causing havoc. Or…" she paused to take a breath, to look at both of us in turn, "… it could all be imagination, which in itself is powerful. People *believed* this place was cursed. Through the centuries they believed that. And so it came to pass. Who knows? I don't. Not really."

"So what are you doing here?" asked Angus. "What are

the duties of an overseer?"

"To restore balance."

Angus looked at me. "It really is as simple as that?" he queried. "Don't you get scared? I mean alone here, at night."

"No, I don't. I keep my imagination in check."

"But what if there really are demons?" he persisted.

"Not within me there aren't. I purged my demons a long time ago. And that's why I'm not scared. They've nothing to seize hold of." Shelley then did what I feared she was going to do; she focused solely on me. "If there is something at the lighthouse, if it's something similar to what was once rife here, you need to tread carefully."

I nodded slowly, wondering if the demons in me were really that easy to see. "The man that used to visit Mr Cameron, could it have been Isaac Leonard himself?"

"In the seventies? No."

"Why not?"

"Because Leonard left Scotland in '67 and died a few years later, in Haiti of all places."

"He died?"

"Yes, his death is well documented, in certain circles anyway. He was dabbling in voodoo by then, no doubt trying to master it as he once attempted to master the dark side here, and being driven insane for his troubles. But I have a theory about that."

"Which is?"

"That he was mad anyway."

I couldn't help but feel the same. "If it wasn't him, then who could it be?"

"No telling, is there? But after it had lain empty for a while, an American couple bought Balskeyne, no doubt thrilled by its bargain price if nothing else, and ran it as a guesthouse until 1980, and if there were any repeat visitors, I'd have to question why."

"Because of the bad vibes?" said Angus.

"Of course," Shelley answered.

"That couple, didn't they feel those vibes too?"

"Maybe they did, maybe they didn't – children are far more sensitive than adults, which is why I knew you were lying instantly when I first met you – there's no way you'd have come back if you'd stayed here when you were younger. On the other hand, it's amazing how oblivious adults can be. One thing I do know is that Leonard still has many devotees, people who make a pilgrimage here. That's why I have to be careful you see. Why I have to run at you, shouting and threatening the odds with the police. I can't let just anyone roam these grounds. It's all about the balance. As long as it exists, I'm safe."

"But at Minch Point, it could be unbalanced?" I said.

"I'm afraid so. And the game you mentioned, Thirteen Ghost Stories, that could have unsettled matters further."

And now, as the property lay empty, that negativity was growing in strength. There was no one to challenge it, if anything it had been encouraged, no matter how unwittingly.

Quickly I came to a decision. "I'm going back there. Tomorrow."

"Are we?" Angus muttered. "I suppose it's about time."

I ignored him, staring at Shelley as she was staring at me – her dark eyes just as penetrating as Eilidh's.

Finally she spoke. "I don't think you're the person for the job."

"Because of my demons?" I said boldly.

"In a way, yes."

"I'm going anyway."

"Can't you come with us?" Angus asked Shelley.

She shook her head. "My place is here."

"Then what's your advice?" I said. "Give us that at least."

"The only advice I can give you is what I suspect you know already. Give what's there nothing to feed on. Because if there is something, if there is a weakness, it will find it."

"*Everyone* has a weakness," I insisted.

"But it's about degrees of weakness. Some of us happen to be content. If you really want my advice, then it's leave, go home! Like I said, you're not the person for the job."

Chapter Seventeen

"HOW dare she! She knows nothing about me."

"She said she's intuitive."

I glared at Angus as I yanked his car door open. "She's presumptuous, that's what she is. I'm not going home, not yet. Just because *she* thinks it's for the best."

"There's no need to get narky with me, Ness. I'm glad you're staying."

My breathing was heavy as Angus turned the engine over. "We need to find out what happened to the Camerons," I muttered, as much to myself as him. "They disappeared, but not into thin air, they went somewhere." I looked up. "I need to get to a phone."

"Why?"

"I want to phone one of my police contacts, see if they can run a search on the Camerons for me."

"You think something bad might have happened to them?"

"It'd be handy to know, one way or the other."

"Okay," Angus replied, nodding. "I'll also ask around, see what I can dig up." He smiled ruefully. "Actually, perhaps that's a poor choice of phrase, considering."

My smile was somewhat rueful too. "I can do this you know."

He held his hands up. "I'm not the one saying you can't, remember?"

That was true, neither him nor his mother. But Shelley... My throat constricted again. She wanted me to give up, because I wasn't at peace with myself as much as she was. Maybe I wasn't, but one thing I had was determination. I'd make sure my efforts paid off.

After she'd 'denounced' me, as I'd interpreted it, Shelley asked if we'd like to take a walk through the grounds.

"Don't expect to sense much though," she'd warned. "I run a tight ship here."

And it was true, I hadn't sensed much at all, a simmering perhaps, a skulking even, something hiding in a corner, plotting and planning, but those plans coming to nothing. I was awed with what she'd achieved, and that annoyed me further.

Before we'd departed, she'd said to me. "You know about white light?"

"Of course," I answered.

"Good intent?"

"Yes, I'll go to the lighthouse with nothing but good intent."

She nodded. "Because even evil needs to be understood."

I remained mute. Was she trying to get at me again?

"You have obsidian in your pocket?"

I gasped. How did she know? Intuitive, that's how. She was damned intuitive.

"Cleanse it regularly," she continued, "by moonlight is best, otherwise in bright sunlight. Prevent any negativity from clinging to it."

"I know, I do." God, I sounded like a petulant child.

"Good."

On the drive back to Skye, the sun re-emerged, but it

was nowhere near as bright as before. Even so, the light was still beautiful, hazy almost. As I stared out of the passenger window again, I had to admit, despite how irked I was, that the balance Shelley was talking about made perfect sense and how easily it could be tipped one way or the other. If it could be maintained, then both sides could coexist, in harmony almost, like night and day – the two opposites, the yin and the yang. It was an intriguing concept, one that consumed me so much I had no idea we'd reached the Kyle until Angus announced it.

"We've a bit of time to kill before the ferry gets here," he continued, "so let's head to the pub, and get that drink we'd promised ourselves. And don't worry; I'm fine with lemonade. Something tells me it's wise to keep a clear head at the moment."

It was – very wise.

"There'll be a phone in the pub too," he added. "If you want to phone that contact of yours."

As soon as we were inside, I did just that, the response I got from my contact being what I'd expected; he'd try and find out about the Camerons, but couldn't promise anything. As he pointed out, some people just didn't want to be found. I was grateful for any help though and, after ringing off, went to buy Angus his drink.

Later, back on Skye, Eilidh had prepared a one-pot vegetable stew complete with dumplings that I realised I was ravenous for, devouring two sizeable helpings. Both Angus and I explained what had happened that day, and I announced my intention to go back to the lighthouse in the morning, breaking it to Angus that I wanted to go alone.

"But—"

"Please," I said, interrupting him. "If I'm alone, it's easier to focus."

"What about the visions? What if you get them again?"

I took a deep breath. "I'll deal with them."

"Really?"

It wasn't just him who raised an eyebrow this time. Eilidh did too.

"I think you should take Angus with you," she said, "as back-up if nothing else."

The irritation I'd felt earlier hadn't quite died down. I had to fight to keep my voice steady. "I thought you both believed in me?"

"We do," they replied, almost in unison.

"Then please, can you trust me on this?"

A moment of silence stretched on and on.

Eilidh eventually spoke. "We trust you."

I exhaled heavily, not realising quite how much I'd needed to hear that.

"You'll be wanting to borrow my car?" Angus asked.

"Yes please, I'll get up early, and go first thing. It's a cleansing I want to perform tomorrow. I'm learning Reiki, so I'll be incorporating that, trying to balance the energy, as Shelley recommended, as well as using psychic persuasion if it's needed."

"You think that's enough?" Eilidh was frowning slightly.

"I think it's a good start. When it's up and running as a guesthouse, that'll be even better. Angus, if you're in charge, it'll be a happy place to visit."

He flashed a shy smile at me. "I hope so."

So did I. Balskeyne had been run as a guesthouse for a period of time too, but what was there, what had been conjured by a man if not mad at the time, certainly on the

brink of madness, still remained, although in a much subdued form, Shelley the overseer, the keeper, the guardian
making sure it stayed that way. I looked at Angus, still with
that shy smile on his face, his red hair as scruffy as ever,
and placed my trust in him too.

* * *

I was thankful for a good night's rest, with no dreams – or
none that I could remember. It wasn't the lighthouse I
drove to first; it was Moira's house, even though all that I'd
sensed there, and the image I'd seen rushing headlong towards the cliff, was residual. Moira may be at peace, but
the negative energy she'd left behind needed cleansing too.
The weather was on my side this time, and the sun was
shining again. It's amazing what a blue sky can do; it can
lift even the dullest of hearts, inspire confidence even. Certainly I felt confident today, despite Shelley, or perhaps *in
spite* of her.

Good thoughts form the backbone of good intent, Ness.

I ought to listen to myself and cleanse my mind too, not
contribute to any negativity.

Moira's house was easy enough to get into. Angus had
secured the door he'd shoved in with his shoulder, but actually it was slightly ajar when I reached it. I was hesitant
for a few seconds and shouted, "Hello, hello," as I entered,
just in case someone was in there – and it could be anyone:
an estate agent perhaps, come to value it at last; a farmer
checking one of his flock hadn't raced in here for shelter
during the storm and then found it couldn't escape when
the more clement weather came. No one answered, and
there were few places to hide. Checking upstairs was empty

too, I returned to the living room and set to work, calling on all four elements – Earth, Air, Fire and Water – to heal and to balance the house. As I'd found before, sadness was the dominant emotion, in the wake of Moira's suicide – I had to fight hard to stop it from overwhelming me again. Afterwards, I sat in Angus's car, in the driver's seat, gripping the steering wheel, just staring out at the cliff top, wondering if I'd see her, the shade of Moira, in perpetual flight. But all there was on the horizon was a flock of sea birds that swooped and soared, freer than I'd ever be, as free as the dead, hopefully.

At last, I put the car into gear and drove to Minch Point Lighthouse, occupying the same parking space that Angus had when we'd visited before. Making my way to the cabin, I stopped briefly to admire a view that I hadn't had the pleasure of seeing previously, thanks to the darkness and the weather. The sea was calm, glittering in the sunlight, and beyond it, there were silhouettes of yet more islands, Lewis and Harris, the Western Isles – their presence on the horizon mythical almost. It was so hard to believe that anything bad could taint such a hallowed spot, but looking at the cabin in front of me, and the lighthouse tower and the keeper's quarter slightly higher on the hill, I'd better believe it, not allow myself to be fooled or sucked in.

The cabin was in worse shape than I'd realised. Its rough rendered walls had big chunks missing, and guttering hung precariously from the roof. All the windows were smashed, as if someone had diligently sat and thrown pebbles at each and every pane. It was hard to swap the majesty of the outside to venture back in there, but that's exactly what I had to do – lay down the foundations for change.

As it was such a tiny dwelling, at least I wasn't in the

cabin for long, half an hour at most, after which I made my way up the gravel path to the main house. Like the cabin, it was painted in white with a buff trim, but coated in the grime of years, the tower that stood beside it a classic piece of maritime architecture. Again I stopped to admire it, almost defiantly this time. Built to be a guiding light, shining brighter than stars in the darkness, how could it have ever failed? It was lonely, a doomed romantic hero mourning the loss of its *raison d'etre*. I felt sad, sadder even than when I'd been in Moira's bedroom. To witness such silent doom was terrible. There was no sound, nothing at all, not the crashing of the waves, or the birds as they'd screeched on that stormy night.

At the front door to where the Camerons had lived, I took all the time I needed to feel grounded, hugging my chunk of obsidian close to my heart. I was about to take a step forward when I thought I did hear something: a shuffling.

It's probably just an animal, darting for cover.

The last thing I needed to do was let my imagination get the better of me – in this scenario it was a weapon too. There'd be some who'd argue that what was happening at the lighthouse was in fact solely the product of over-imaginative minds. I envied that view. If you held no belief in the spiritual world, could it ever harm you? The American couple that had run Balskeyne as a guesthouse might well have been protected, purely because of their disbelief. On the other hand, if you did believe, if you *knew*...

Deciding to stop philosophising and get on with the job, I entered the main building. All was still inside. The first thing I did was cross over to the windows, pulling aside or yanking down what curtains remained. The difference was immediate – the gloom losing some of its opaqueness. I tried to open the windows next, but they were all stuck and, unlike at the cabin, the glass panes were intact. Deciding to rectify that, I picked up a stool and, utilising one of its wooden legs, took great delight in smashing a few. I really wouldn't consider myself a vandal, but there's a saying: needs must when the devil drives. It was essential to change the air inside this place, not let it fester any longer.

Having done all this, it was time to begin the ritual cleansing, again harnessing the power of the natural elements, which were so abundant on Skye. Kicking a tide of debris out of my way as I walked, I was surprised not just how calm I was, but at how calm it was in the lodgings too. Things were different in daylight; I knew that, but *so* different?

Visualising myself as well as this entire structure at Minch Point blanketed in a white glow, I practised the symbol of *Cho Ku Rei,* enticing the power of the universe to enter this domain, to reside here, and for balance to be restored. Throughout the entire area downstairs I practised this symbol, feeling the power of my energy, and how it flowed, creating another shield against the threat of attack. Having finished downstairs, I climbed the stairs, any trepidation I harboured successfully packaged up and stowed away. I repeated the process in the main bedroom, Niall's bedroom, and finally headed to Caitir's bedroom. My breathing still deep and even, I pushed the door wider, *Cho Ku Rei, Cho Ku Rei* repeating in a loop in my mind. It was so quiet inside, the curtains closed at the window, which I opened straightaway. Rather than break another windowpane, I struggled with the sash. Eventually I managed to open it an inch or two, imagining fresh air like a Pac-Man, rushing in, and devouring all that was stale. I turned around and walked to the centre of the room. There were several candle stubs on the floor, along with glass jars that had once housed them, most broken, but some intact. There was general litter too, left behind from many teenage gatherings, even an item of clothing – a girl's red cardigan – which I picked up and handled, checking for any vibes that might still cling to it. There were none and so I dropped it.

Benign; it was all quite benign.

Chanting out loud, I called on the universe to work with me, not against me. If black magic had been practised here, then white magic was going to cancel it out.

"And soon there'll be life here again, lots of energy, love and laughter. Because of that, any negativity will diminish, become insubstantial. Whatever you are, I'm not afraid of you, I'm the *antithesis* of you, and my word is true. You do not belong here in any significance. If you've been conjured by vain, inglorious men, I'm sorry for that. But you cannot stay."

Resolutely, I stood there – a lone challenger. If it attacked, if it tried to force-feed me a diet of terrible visions designed to bring me to knees, it wouldn't work. Last time I hadn't known that would happen. This time I'd closed my mind against such infiltration. My lack of fear would be the thing that would frustrate it, that and my belief in myself. I *could* do this. That was the entire reason I possessed this gift – to help. If I could help, it made sense of it; it helped me to cope with how different I was.

Different?

Ness, shut up, don't think anymore…

It *had* to be the reason – if not, then why? So much

persecution it had cost me, by strangers as well as those that were supposed to love me, my family…

Ness!

But it was true; I *had* been persecuted. Only now, in my mid-twenties, was I coming into my own, doing things like this, standing in an abandoned house, one that was reputedly haunted, the smell of something sickly sweet in the air, the haven of mice, rats, spiders – and me. It was laughable, so damned funny, so why wasn't I smiling?

You'd think I'd be smiling.

NESS!

I blinked, came to, shaking my head vigorously. What had just happened to me? I'd gone into a reverie of some kind, negative thoughts doing their utmost to entrap me.

Breathing slowly in and out, I clenched and unclenched my fists. This thing, it was clever, I'd give it that. It was canny.

"Even so, I'm not frightened of you," I reiterated, "or the games that you play, because that's all they are. And all games must come to an end."

Laughter! I definitely heard laughter. Was someone here after all?

I darted forward in the direction I'd heard it – the hallway – and looked from side to side.

Breathe, Ness. Keep your cool.

In case someone was hiding – someone living that is – I called out, just as I'd done in Moira's house. "Is there anyone here?"

No reply, but my sense that someone was spying on me intensified.

"If there is, show yourself!"

And have a good laugh at my expense. How can I blame

you? Look how stupid I am, an idiot, trying to face a demon on my own, to fight it. How can I ever hope to succeed, when I'm just as bad? When I'm a demon too? I'd have to be to do what I did, to cause so much shame, more than I'd caused already. Officially mad, that's what I was. How can I continue to deny it? I'm not worthy. I'm a freak. I'm the one who should be banished.

As though I'd received a blow to the stomach, I doubled over, the bitterness of bile scorching my throat. I hadn't been physically attacked, but I almost wished I had, it would be far easier to bear. Those thoughts, they weren't mine, surely they weren't. They'd simply formed in my head, sentences running on and on, crashing into one another. I had to get out. There was nothing benign about this place, or what was in it.

Oh, look, poor me, feeling sorry for myself, I can't seem to stop. I'm always feeling sorry for myself, I'm such a victim, such a martyr, a curse, and an abomination. I can't even bear to think of what I did, to acknowledge it. And at such a young age too. Thirteen, only thirteen. Of course it would have to be: a cursed age for a cursed child.

Doing my utmost to straighten up, I ran for the stairs, practically blind with tears. I only wished I could shut off my hearing too, silence that laughter, which wasn't mine, but was so like mine. I could hear it still and knew without doubt it would soon turn to wailing – something I couldn't bear to hear, not again, not after I'd tried for so long to shut it out.

"You're dead," I hissed, "you and mum both."

At the top of the stairs I hesitated. Was there someone at the bottom, a crone-like figure, staring up at me? I wiped at my eyes. Although I'd torn the curtains down, although it was barely noon, there was so much darkness – obscuring the figure, or hiding it. One minute it was there, the next it wasn't. Would it reappear when I got halfway? Would it fly at me, and smother me with the weight of hell as I lay screaming?

I had to control my imagination. There's nothing there, nothing!

Why am I denying it? Why am I pretending? For so long, I used to say the same thing: there's nothing there, nothing. Try and convince myself. But there always was. Always. 'Only a witch can see what you can see, an evil, stinking witch.' That's what she told me once, that bitch of a mother, that crone. 'And you know what happens to witches, don't you? No? Well you should. We rid the world of them. We don't want them.'

"For God's sake, stop this," I cry, feeling in the grip of madness more than I ever had. The laughter was changing, just as it had done in my dream last night, no longer soft and sweet, it was becoming more stilted, a sob creeping in, becoming more pronounced.

If I stayed here…

I couldn't. It knew my weakness too well.

Having checked the bottom of the stairs again, that there was no one lurking, I practically threw myself down the steps, praying I wouldn't fall, land in a heap and injure myself. If I did, I really would be at the mercy of what was here. It could toy with me further, take its time, and really enjoy the game. Thankfully, I reached the bottom in one piece, refusing to look anywhere but ahead, hurtling myself forward as the wailing began.

Pain shot through my fragile heart.

At the front door, I grabbed the handle and yanked it open. Again, I couldn't believe what I was seeing: the weather, so beautiful before, had turned – either mourning alongside me or mocking me. Such hard rain they have in Scotland, the clouds closing in, encircling me – a shield wall, so much more effective than the one I'd built.

The car, I had to find it, get out of here, and not be stranded. The thought of being stranded…

Coward. I can add that to my list of glowing attributes. I'm a born coward.

I wouldn't listen anymore, I refused to – those were not my thoughts, they were being planted in my head. Or were they? Because I *had* thought along those lines before, many times, thoughts like that had once plagued me. I pressed forwards through the rain, my eyes peeled for the car. Where the heck was it? A little green Fiesta, not new, but as scruffy as anything, as its owner. Would Angus be safe here in the future, the guardian of Minch Point Light-house? Would anyone? There it was! The car hadn't been spirited away as I'd half-expected, it was where I'd left it. I felt in my pocket for the key, found the chunk of obsidian, retrieved it and held it to my chest again, drawing what comfort I could, but it was the key I needed. That was in the other pocket. Thank God.

In the car, it took several attempts to insert the key into the ignition, my hands were shaking so much, but finally I succeeded. Quickly putting it into reverse, I pressed my foot to the floor, the tyres screeching. Back on the road, I drove away, taking bends and corners at the speed only a native would. As I drove, another thought occurred, this one very much my own: the cabin, the gravel path leading up to the house, the *west-facing* house, and the isolated location: it had exactly the same qualities as Balskeyne.

Chapter Eighteen

IF I'd hoped to find respite at Eilidh's house, I was wrong. As soon as I entered the front door, I sensed commotion, even a non-psychic would have been able to – the atmosphere so tense you could slice through it with a knife. Hurrying up the hallway, I heard voices coming from the dining room, several of them, speaking in hushed but agitated tones. Sure enough, when I stood at the threshold, I found not just Eilidh and Angus in situ; Craig's father, Mr Ludmore, was also present and another man, that I hadn't yet met.

Seeing me, Angus shot to his feet. "Ness! You're all right! I was about to borrow Ben's car and drive out to the lighthouse to look for you."

"I… erm… who's Ben?" I asked.

The man who was a stranger to me stood too. "That's me, Ben Mowbray, I'm Amy's father, one of the teenagers who was at the lighthouse the night something happened to Ally, happened to them all. The thing is, Ally's taken a turn for the worse. She and her parents are at the medical centre in Broadford, waiting to be taken to Raigmore on the mainland. That's when they can move Ally that is."

"When? Why? How has she got worse?" My own predicament shelved, I wanted to know as much as possible.

"When did she deteriorate?"

"Sit down, lass." It was Eilidh. "You looked flummoxed enough when you entered the room, let alone after. We'll tell you everything and then... we'll decide what to do about it."

What had happened was even worse than I thought. Molly had heard banging and crashing coming from Ally's room, not an unusual occurrence – she'd already told us that Ally was sometimes given to fits of rage – but this time it was accompanied with the most terrible screaming. Her husband was at home too and both of them rushed upstairs to find out what was happening. Ally hadn't barricaded herself in this time; on the contrary, she'd left the door open. They rushed inside and that's when Ally attacked them. She had a knife, which she managed to stab her mother with before her father got her under control.

"She stabbed her mother?" I gasped. "How badly is she hurt?"

"Not badly, thank goodness," Ben replied. "It's an arm wound, but she'll be going to Raigmore for treatment nonetheless. I live along the road from them; I was passing, on my way to the village, when I heard the commotion. After having to bash the front door down, I raced up the stairs, made my way to where all the noise was coming from and I'll tell you, the sight that met me... All I could do for a few seconds was stand and stare." He shook his head, clearly still in shock. "They were always such a normal family, the Dunns, a *nice* family, you know? What's happened to them, to all of our kids? I don't understand it. In Ally's room, the walls were covered in the number thirteen. She'd written it everywhere. I've heard that some of the others have done that too, och, not on the walls or anything, but on paper. They sit there and they write it over and over. It's like they're obsessed."

As I'd been in my dream – obsessed or possessed – what was the difference?

Mr Mowbray continued to speak. "John was struggling with Ally, I mean really struggling. It was wrong, all wrong, he's a big bloke, and she's just a wee thing. He yelled at me to call an ambulance, so I had to leave them and rush back downstairs, but I could hear Ally screaming all the while, and not just screaming, she was saying stuff too."

My breathing becoming more rapid, I was unable to calm it; I didn't even bother to try this time. "What was she saying?"

"Something along the lines of *'It's won. We played the game and it's won.'* What could she mean by that? What on earth could she mean? I'm telling you that girl was bucking and kicking, she was foaming at the mouth. And when I got home, Amy, my own kid, had locked herself in her room too, as if she knew what had happened, although I hadn't yet told anyone. She was crying, inconsolably. My wife and I, we tried our best with her, even our dog, Smokie, sat by her door, howling away as if pleading to be let in, but she just kept on crying. And then she stopped and said something, something which raised the hairs on my arms." He paused again, looking as if he was about to start crying himself. Instead he clamped his lips into a tight white line before continuing. "She also said 'It's won'. The same words Ally used. *Who's* won? What's going on? I came here because I'd heard you were investigating the case, that you're a psychic. I need to know what's going on!"

"I don't know the full picture," I admitted, "not yet. But

it's far from good."

His complexion was grey almost. "Don't tell me they've summoned the devil?"

I was eager to dispel that notion. "I think it's more likely they've tuned into negative energy of some description, and it's... erm... a force to be reckoned with."

"I told Amy not to go to the lighthouse," he said, such despair in his voice, "to stay away. But would she listen? Do teenagers *ever* listen? And that game, that stupid game... Why do they do that, try and spook themselves? How can we put an end to this... I don't know... spell that they're under? How do we reverse it? Play the game again?"

About to say no, I stopped. What he'd suggested made a dreadful kind of sense.

Looking at each of them in turn, noting the fear and confusion that had begun to haunt them, I finally gave an answer. "I think we should do exactly that; beat it at its own game."

Chapter Nineteen

ANGUS had grown pale, and Eilidh was clutching at the collar of the dress she wore. My agreement with Ben had shocked them, but Ben – a parent of one of the teenagers afflicted, a girl who was barely sixteen – looked hopeful, and that spurred me on.

"We'd have to exercise the utmost care," I explained, "perform some rituals of our own before we enter the lighthouse en masse again. I don't want you to be alarmed by that; it's not black magic. It's working with the universe, and drawing on the light to protect us."

"I'm not alarmed," Ben said. "Pardon my language, but I want to beat this fucker at its own game. And believe me, I'll do what it takes."

"But will your daughter?" I asked, wary of putting traumatised kids under more pressure.

"We need to hold a meeting," Eilidh declared, "with all those who've been involved. See who's willing to help and who isn't. And if they're not…"

"If they're not, some of us will take their place," Angus insisted. "In memory of Moira."

I smiled at him. "In memory of Moira."

Eilidh stood, brushed the front of her dress down and then clasped her hands in front of her. "There's a community hall near Dunvegan, that's central enough for everyone I think. Angus and Ben, can you see who's willing to come to the meeting?" She checked her watch. "It's nearing two, we need to get on. How about we set a time of five o' clock?"

"It's doable," Angus said, "if Ben and I leave now. There are eleven families other than the Dunns to speak to, we could divide them between us, Ben?"

"Aye, that's fine, everyone needs to know what's happened to Ally."

"Ben," I reiterated, "it's imperative that no one goes to the lighthouse under duress, only those that are reasonably confident. If they all decline, fair enough, I'll find another way."

"If they all decline?" Ben repeated and then he laughed, a booming sound that startled all of us. "You're in the Highlands, lassie, we don't breed wimps up here. There'll be very few that decline, you'll see. You cannae play Thirteen Ghost Stories on your own."

A short while later, with Angus and Ben dispatched, I was ruminating on that thought. Could I ensure the safety of those who chose to go back to Minch Point? Was it reckless of me to even think so? What if it put them all in the line of danger? More danger, that is, than they were already in. After all, if Ally had worsened, so could the others. No one was safe, not really, no matter where they were – at home or at the lighthouse.

Eilidh came up behind me. "It's a heavy load, isn't it?"

"What? Erm... I suppose. Oh, what the hell... Yes, yes it is. To tell you the truth, Eilidh, I don't know what to do for the best."

Pulling up a chair so that she could sit beside me, she

took my hands in hers, her skin felt like velvet, but despite that, her grip was firm. "Ben's right in what he says, we're a hardy lot that live here, but for all that, we're spiritual too, you can't help but be."

"Angus said something similar," I replied. "He called this God's own country."

She nodded. "Aye, and it is, but if we're close to God, maybe the devil's close too."

"It's so hard to believe, isn't it? It's so beautiful here."

"But it's wrathful too, when the weather sets in."

Remembering what had happened at the lighthouse, I agreed. "It can certainly turn on a sixpence. One minute the sun's shining, the next there's another storm on the horizon."

"Four seasons in one day, that's how it goes on Skye. Look," – releasing a soft breath, she leant forward – "something's happening here, we can't deny it, try as we might. We can't hide from it either. And so what choice is there, but to face it head on?"

"But I'm worried about people getting hurt... more people that is. Ally stabbed her mum for goodness' sake, she could have killed her, or turned the knife on herself."

"I know, I know. I don't think any of us are going to take this lightly, dear, believe me."

"I know that. You're good people, all of you."

She smiled. "Surely that's something in our favour?"

I smiled too. "I just... Like you said, it's a lot of responsibility. If it goes wrong, and I can't guarantee that it won't, the buck stops with me."

"I'll not blame you, lass, or Angus, or any of the folks that I know." She released my hand and sat back. "Och, but I bet you wish there were two of you sometimes, don't you?"

For a brief moment I could only stare at her. "What did you say?"

The phone rang, a shrill sound that startled me again.

Still smiling, Eilidh eased herself out of her chair. "I'd best answer that," she said, leaving the dining room and heading into the hallway.

I barely had time to think before she was back. "It's for you. It's the police."

"The police? Oh, it must be Dan; he's with the Sussex Police. I asked him to run a trace on the Camerons. Sorry, I gave him this number to contact me, I hope that's okay."

"Of course it's okay. Come on, don't keep him waiting."

I hurried into the hallway, eager to hear what Dan had to say. When I returned to the dining room, Eilidh was looking as grave as I felt.

"It's bad news, is it?"

"The worst," I answered.

The Camerons were dead, all four of them. Mr Cameron had shot his family and then himself eight years ago, on another remote island, this one off the coast of Ireland.

* * *

Despite Ben and Eilidh assuring me there'd be a big turnout at the community hall, there wasn't. There was Mr and Mrs Ludmore and their son Craig, Ben of course, with his wife, Caroline, and their daughter, Amy. Also in attendance were Isabel and her parents, Grant and his parents, a young lad known as Denny with his mother and father, and another girl, called Elaine or Lainey, as she preferred. She was there with her mother, Diane. Other parents had been talked to, but declined getting involved further, as had their teenage offspring. I guess there are some things even the hardiest of folks can't face. I could sympathise with that. Ben started to apologise for the turnout, but I stopped him.

"There's enough for us to do what we have to."

And we did *have* to, I saw that now, the deaths of the Camerons had clarified that for me. I was still reeling from the information that Dan had imparted. Mr Cameron had shot his entire family and then turned the gun on himself? For no obvious reason? Where they'd been living, Arranmore, with a population of roughly around five hundred according to Dan, and in a cottage, not a lighthouse, they'd done more or less what they'd done on Skye, and kept themselves to themselves, not mixed at all. "The fella I talked to that dealt with the case told me that fellow islanders described the family as weird," Dan had said. "The general consensus amongst them was that Cameron wasn't a man to be messed with, that he only had to look at you and you'd start shaking. The .22 rifle he used was registered to him."

I'd asked Dan about the kids, Caitir and Niall, and whether that same man had said anything about them.

"Only that they were a pitiful sight, in death I mean. They looked half-starved, as did their mother. Not him though, he was a big man, he obviously ate well enough."

"Poor kids," I'd responded, "his poor wife." I'd never known them, I'd only ever heard of them, but that didn't stop my heart aching for them. They were victims in more ways than one. Even though the news was gruesome, it didn't make me want to run away and take the next train headed south, removing myself from this lonely land and what dwelt in it. My *friends* also dwelt here. That's how I'd come to think of Eilidh and Angus. Together, we had to try and finish what had been started so many years before.

In the hall, it was Ben who kicked off proceedings, explaining who I was to those who hadn't yet met me, and also what we intended to do.

"There's no pressure on anyone to go back to the lighthouse," he said. "We've been quite clear about that, but we also think it's the only way to eradicate this thing."

"And if not eradicate it," I added a touch more cautiously, "to subdue it."

The usual questions were asked. 'Is it the devil?' 'Are you really psychic?' 'What if we play and it wins again, if, like Ally, we end up losing our minds?'

"We'll win this time," I said in response to such questions. "And when we do, that will help Ally too; it will tame whatever's in her. An important thing to remember is that we're going in fully prepared, we're not blind anymore. Our *expectation* is to win. Believe it."

"It can't be that simple," someone said, Denny's father I think.

I inclined my head towards him. "You think it's that simple, do you, to believe in yourself? It isn't. Sometimes, it's the hardest thing of all."

He pondered that, opened his mouth to respond, but clearly decided against it.

"You mentioned something about protection procedures," Ben reminded me. "What did you mean?"

"More magic?" someone else muttered before I could respond.

"It's not magic," I said, reiterating what I'd said to Ben earlier today. "It's working in harmony with the earth's natural energies, an holistic practice if you like, and partly rooted in an ancient practice called Reiki, which I'm learning at the moment."

"Learning?" It was Lainey's mother who questioned this. "You're not an expert?"

Eilidh stepped in. "Diane, there are some things that take a lifetime to learn. I can vouch for Ness, she does have psychic ability, but more than that, she has a good heart. That's what really matters when you're dealing with something like this."

I was grateful for the support. "Eilidh's right, but drawing on universal energy does help, and we all need to do that. Imagine the purest white light you can, coming straight at you from source, and wrapping itself around you. This is your armour – keep it in place. We also need to go in with good intent. Whatever's there, however dark it is, it's to be pitied, rather than feared." Drawing on what Shelley had said, I added, "We can't rid ourselves of negative energy entirely, it's unrealistic to think that, but what we can do is restore balance. The plans that Angus's uncle has for the lighthouse are a good thing – they'll help to *maintain* balance. When we're done, when the builders have moved in, when there's life at the lighthouse once again, it'll be a good place to visit; one where happy memories are forged, where there's conversation and laughter. All that will help."

"So why are we doing anything?" asked Mrs Ludmore. "Why don't we just encourage Angus's uncle to get started as soon as he can?"

"Because of Ally," Angus said. "This thing is becoming more powerful, so we have to try and break it while we can, not wait for sales negotiations to be completed."

"But why Ally? Why did it pick on her so bad?"

Craig had posed the question, but it was Isabel who answered. "Maybe it was because she'd just found out she was adopted."

There was a sharp intake of breath in the room, and a few people looked at each other; their eyes wide with surprise. "Was she?" asked one.

"Aye," Isabel continued, "and she found out by accident. She was looking for something and came across the papers. They were going to tell her at some point, but I think it was her mam who kept putting it off. She told Ally that it didn't matter, she was their child, and they were her parents, in all the ways that mattered. There was a big hooha and Ally was distraught, but I thought they'd sorted it out. What happened at the lighthouse, it wasn't long after that, and Ally had been drinking – a lot. She never usually drinks." Isabel looked at her parents, "And neither do I by the way, before you start."

But no one started. If anything, everyone appeared dumbstruck.

"I'd never have guessed," said Ben finally. "She actually looks like them."

"Och, away with you," his wife replied. "As Molly said, she's theirs, in all the ways that count. I can understand it's difficult to break the news, why you'd keep putting it off. You don't want your child to love you any the less, do you, just because of biology, or rather the lack of it?"

Various murmurs of agreement floated around the room.

"Look," I said, "I haven't got all the answers to the situation we've found ourselves in, but Angus is right when he says that what's there is gaining in power. I went to the lighthouse today to perform a basic cleansing, and, well, let's just say, it's clever, this thing and what it can do – it has intelligence, no matter how basic. From what I understand, especially in the light of what I've just learnt about Ally, it plays on your weaknesses, your sorrows, and your fears, it unearths them. If any of you feel vulnerable in any way, then please don't come. If you're going to do this, you have to do it in the right frame of mind."

"What happens if we don't come with you?" Again it was Diane who asked.

"Then I go alone."

"Erm… hang on a minute, you don't get rid of me that easy," Angus looked as if he was going to breathe fire through his nostrils. "I'm coming too. I've told you."

"Thanks." It was all I could say. I *would* go back to the lighthouse alone, but the truth is I didn't want to. As thirteen had proved, there's strength in numbers.

"Well… in that case, Lainey," said Dianne, "what do you think? It's entirely up to you."

Lainey was a pretty girl, as dark-haired as myself, her skin just as white. She hesitated, but not for long. "I'm going back, Mum. If there's a chance we can stop this, then I'm taking it. It is getting worse, that lady's right. And lately, there've been visions."

"And urges." It was Grant speaking, a boy with hair as red as Angus's. "That's recent too. I've the urge to hurt someone." He shook his head. "The hours I spend in my bedroom, sitting on my hands, trying to stop that urge. Mum, Dad, I'm scared for us. Ally's a great girl, as gentle as they come, the fact that she attacked her parents…" He paused, as if trying to understand such a heinous fact. "Even despite what she'd just found out, she wouldn't do stuff like that, not normally. But there's this voice, it whispers in your ear, it tells you to hurt as many people as you can, and it's getting louder. Just lately it's not a whisper anymore, it's more like a command." Suddenly he lunged himself into his mother's arms, who was sitting right beside him. "I'd never do what Ally did, Mum, Dad. I'd never hurt you. I love you. I'm sorry. I don't want to think this way, but it's making me."

His mother didn't even hesitate; immediately she comforted him, told him that she loved him too, more than anything. His father joined in, all of them hugging, clinging on to each other as if their lives depended on it. Seeing such a display of emotion, other teenagers in the room turned to their parents too, their parents reaching out just as readily to them. It was something wonderful to see – the love that they all had for each other and once again I was filled with hope. Love was stronger than hate. Love got things done.

But hate's powerful too, Ness. Whoever loved you like that?

The thought formed before I could stop it, but I couldn't disagree with it, not when it was true. Before I could think any further, Eilidh stood up and made her way towards me.

"Eilidh?" I questioned.

She didn't answer, she simply stopped in front of me and held out her arms. I felt awkward, unsure how to respond.

"Go on," Angus nudged me. "She wants a hug. And afterwards, so do I."

I stared at him too, somewhat aghast.

"Go on," he said again.

Still feeling awkward, I stood up, a hesitant smile on my

face. It was Eilidh who closed the gap between us, enfolding me in her arms. Again, there was such strength in her embrace. At once the tears started, I couldn't stop them. How awful to cry like this, in a room full of people. But it was also cathartic. She was giving me something I'd craved all my life – acceptance and love: *motherly* love.

"This is something your mother should have done too," she whispered in my ear. "If I'd had the privilege of being your mother, I know I would have."

And there it was – *if* she'd been my mother. Sometimes we luck out. Sometimes we don't. Is it right to think you're unlovable because of an accident of birth? I wondered. Was it time, aged twenty-five, to put all that had happened behind me? God knows I'd tried.

Luckily everyone else around the room seemed preoccupied with each other, no one noticed what was happening with me, except Angus. He stood too and hugged me and then all three of us hugged together.

"You can do this," Eilidh said.

"Try telling that to Shelley," I replied, looking wryly at Angus, but he was looking elsewhere, towards the entrance of the hall. As he pulled away, I frowned.

"You can tell her yourself," he said.

Chapter Twenty

I swung round. Shelley stood at the hall entrance, dressed in identical clothing to yesterday, surveying the scene before her. Slowly, leisurely, her gaze travelled towards me. There was something in her eyes, what was it? Approval? Dared I even think it?

Angus hurried over to stand by her side. A few others had noticed she was there and were nudging each other, whispering.

"This is Shelley," Angus announced. "I asked her if she'd come today and, well, I'm grateful that she has."

I looked at Angus stunned, when had he taken her telephone number? I hadn't even thought to do that.

"Shelley's the overseer at Balskeyne," he continued, "which, as some of you know, is a house on the banks of Loch Ness, the one that used to belong to the Black Magician, Isaac Leonard."

"And Robbie Nelson," Craig piped up. "Such a great band, The Ridge."

"Overseer?" His father questioned. "The caretaker you mean?"

"He means exactly that," Shelley announced, her imperious tone holding everybody's attention. "The house burnt down last year, a kitchen fire. I don't know if any of you were aware of that?" Several shakes of the head confirmed that people hadn't been. "There's no reason why you should, really," Shelley continued. "I'm glad none of you have a lingering interest in the house, except of course," and here she smiled at Craig, "as the former dwelling of a rock star. Angus tells me you're all planning on going back to the lighthouse, to play Thirteen Ghost Stories, to beat the negative energy that's in residence at its own game. I have to admit there's logic in that." Eyeing me, she added, "An *impressive* logic. Even so, I was concerned, and that's why I came tonight, to see how people felt about this. I walk in and... you're all hugging. That's good, very good. Who's going back?"

"Me!"

"We are."

"All of us I think."

The answers came thick and fast.

"And you're all going with the intention of helping each other as well as yourselves?" Shelley asked. "Ally Dunn in particular?"

"Aye."

"Yes."

"Of course."

Again, there was a barrage of answers.

"Because it's real what you're up against," she warned. "But it's not invincible. There are some in this world that will have you think otherwise, but they'd be trying to frighten you. The dark is not as strong as the light. Light has the upper hand."

There were several nods of agreement.

She gestured to me, putting my nerves on edge a little. I agreed with all she'd said so far, but what was she intending to say about me? Keeping my gaze steady, I bit on my lip as she spoke. "Leading you all is this young woman. I want you to listen to her, to do as she says, because she's the real deal, she knows what she's talking about."

Whilst I gazed at her in wonder, she added, "If you don't mind, everyone, I'd like to have a private word with Ness and then I'll be on my way. Good luck to you all."

"Why can't you come?" Isabel's father seemed as awe-struck by her presence as I was.

"Because my place is at Balskeyne," she explained. "I can't stay away for too long. And also because," she inclined her head towards me, "Ness is more than capable."

As she approached me, I was battling confusion. Yester-day she'd said one thing and now – in Dunvegan's com-munity hall – she was saying quite another.

Before I could question her about this, she leant into me, her voice low, conspiratorial, "Ever heard of reverse psychology?"

"Reverse…? I'm not sure I know what you mean."

"If someone says you can't do something, it only serves to make you want to do it more. Some people anyway. There are those that will take heed of what you say, will see it as a get out clause, seize the opportunity and run."

"So it was a test?" I said, slightly annoyed.

"Which you passed with flying colours."

"You really are blunt."

"I see no harm in that. Not in these circumstances."

My annoyance faded. "Fair point."

All around us, people were huddled together in small groups, although a few kept glancing over to where I stood with Shelley, especially Angus, who looked as if he was going to burst with curiosity. Some were pulling their coats on, or tightening scarves, and I realised something: we couldn't delay any longer; we had to go tonight, whilst morale was high. If we put it off, perhaps waited until the next day, it would give fear a chance to creep back in, to find the cracks in these people, and strangle their hearts and minds.

"That's right," Shelley said, "seize the moment. Tonight is best."

I stared at her. "Intuition, right?"

"If I'm honest with you, Ness, it doesn't take a genius to work out the way your thoughts are running. I can read your intentions well enough in your eyes, and by the expression on your face. But listen, I've more information for you that may prove vital. The person who used to come and visit Cameron, he was, as I thought, and as you suspected, a devotee of Isaac Leonard, a disciple if you like."

I inhaled. "How do you know?"

"Because Donder McKendrick told me."

"Donder? I've heard of him before."

"He was the lighthouse keeper before Cameron, he's now a taxi driver, lives close to me, on the banks of Loch Ness. He's an old guy but he's still working. I don't think he'll ever stop. After the isolation of working at Minch Point, he's gone the other way; loves the company of people. In many ways, although he doesn't acknowledge it, not consciously anyway, he's an overseer too, or at least he was. He kept balance at the lighthouse, kept the darkness at bay, in a literal sense and just by being who he was, a good man, a kind man, always with the welfare of others at the heart of everything he did. You see, Minch Point, it's not too dissimilar to Balskeyne—"

"It has the same dimensions," I blurted out, "as Balskeyne I mean, those that were needed for the spell."

"Does it?" She asked the question, but there was no surprise in it. "I've not been so I wouldn't know, but it fits with what I'm about to tell you. The land that Minch Point is built on is drenched in blood too. The ship that was wrecked there, in 1909, just after the lighthouse was built, claimed the lives of so many innocents, just as the fire in the church did at Balskeyne, remember?"

I nodded.

"Sometimes, when there's death on that scale, when there's so many emotions involved, all of them steeped in fear, it forms an imprint, an attraction. It serves to *alert* energies that are similar. When Donder handed over the lighthouse to Cameron, he thought him a fine and upstanding man; those are the words he used. He'd come from Barra with his family, no stranger to peace and quiet, not one to be unsettled by it, to be driven mad. On the contrary, he seemed keen to perform his duties; Donder sensed nothing wrong with him at all. Sometime later, he gave a lift to someone who was staying at Balskeyne; he wanted to go all the way to the lighthouse, to speak to the man who runs it. On the way there, he told Donder the purpose of his visit. He had a proposal for the keeper, that's what he said. What that proposal was, he didn't elaborate, and Donder was too polite to ask. But Donder took him several times to the lighthouse after that, over a period of weeks, that's how long he must have stayed at Balskeyne, and on one of those occasions, Cameron came to the car, where Donder would wait to take the man home again, to see his visitor off. He told me he was shocked to see the change in him, he was surly, gruff, barely even acknowledged Donder. In contrast, every time Cameron looked at his visitor, he seemed dazzled, as if he were staring into the face of a God. The fares to the lighthouse eventually ceased and Donder was glad. He never liked his passenger, or his enigmatic conversations. One thing he did though, he asked the man his full name – before that he only knew his forename – and when I spoke to him this morning, he managed to recall it without hesitation: Jonathan Grey. I did some more phoning, some more digging, as there are those in my circles that might know such a name."

"And?"

"And someone did: a woman who lives in the south, close to where you live, in Hastings. She's a talented psychic, so is her daughter, Jessica." She paused. "She explained that Grey was an Occultist, one known to have rented a house on Skye, which is probably why the taxi rides finally came to an end. Donder, knowing Skye so well, as well as everyone on the west coast, knew exactly where it was that he'd stayed. He'd also heard what happened to Moira. When we were discussing it, it became clear that all three houses formed a triangle, with Grey's at the pinnacle."

"A triangle?"

"That's right, for added occult measure. Like the number thirteen, a triangle has significance too, it represents a merging of the spiritual and earthly realms."

"Another reason why Moira was perhaps affected?"

Shelley agreed. "She was implicated without even knowing it."

"Combine that with LSD…"

"And it doesn't bear thinking about."

"I wonder if he was her supplier?"

"Grey?" Shelley questioned. "You'd have to work it out, and see if the dates tally, but you can find a peddler of drugs anywhere in the world, in places even more remote than this. I was in Borneo once, deep in the jungle… " She paused. "But that's a story for another time. Concerning Grey's house, I took a detour there this evening, there's a *For Sale* sign outside it, I don't know how long it's been up for sale, or indeed how long he stayed on Skye, but the sign is as decrepit as the house itself, creaking on its hinges as the wind blows around it. As for its aura, even the most hardened cynic would be able to sense something wrong. I doubt anyone will ever buy it. In fact, I know they won't."

"You know? How?"

"Because on my way back to Balskeyne, I shall visit the house again and set fire to it, thereby breaking the chain. It will help in your endeavour. It will help a lot."

My eyes widened as my mouth dropped. "But what if you get caught?" I whispered. "There's already been a fire at Balskeyne, what if people put two and two together?"

She gestured around her. "These people? You really think they'd turn me in?"

"Erm… no." Of course they wouldn't, not given the circumstances, they'd close the net. As for the people who owned the house, perhaps in some way they'd be glad too. What had been tainted, would be cleansed, and the land more valuable because of it. "Thank you," I added.

"Believe me, the pleasure is all mine."

I thought back to the supposed kitchen fire at Balskeyne. "Is that the fate of the lighthouse too? If all else fails, I burn it to the ground."

"You won't fail, you know what you're up against. As

I've said before, this conjuring needs to be subdued, and a guardian set in place."

"Angus. He'll be in place soon."

"A good choice. He's a good lad. Fond of you it seems."

"He's twenty-three!"

"And you're a young head on old shoulders, I get it."

"What happened to Jonathan Grey? Did your contact know? Is he still at large?"

"No. He did leave here at some point, ending up in Brighton. And there he was discovered, in the early eighties, in a grimy little bedsit with his head blown off."

"He was murdered?"

"Like his master, he'd committed suicide. You can't get that close to darkness and remain sane."

I swallowed, digesting this before revealing what else I knew. "The Camerons are all dead too, Mr Cameron shot his wife and kids and then himself. That was in '79."

"It doesn't surprise me."

"So much death," I mutter, swallowing again.

"In the Camerons' case, it might help to think of it as release."

It was certainly a more preferable angle. "And you're certain about this, are you? That Grey ensnared Cameron somehow, that maybe he plied him with promises of magnificent riches if he helped him with his work, with his spell. It does seem to fit, but—"

"I'm certain," she replied. "Call it intuition."

As she smiled so did I, but it was with difficulty, the gravitas of what she'd said – *You can't get that close to darkness and remain sane* – weighed heavily.

Shelley laid her hand on my arm. "You *are* the person for the job."

"Am I?" My voice was nothing but a whisper.

"Yes. But for reasons that I wish weren't so."

I frowned, puzzled by her words, but fearing to ask – and she knew it. Her expression softened as she took pity on me. In many ways she reminded me of Eilidh: such a good person at heart. "All you really need in this situation is love. There's plenty of that here."

She was right, there was.

"And forgiveness," she added. "Forgiveness is good too. If you can, that is…"

Chapter Twenty-One

SHELLEY went her way and the rest of us went ours. I was right: morale was high, everybody piled into their respective cars, not to go to the lighthouse, not initially, but to various houses to collect the equipment that we'd need for the night – torches, plenty of them, candles and tealights, thick jumpers and jackets, lots of them too, and bin bags for clearing the rubbish. Everywhere in the lighthouse there were glass bottles and other items that could be used as weapons; we needed them gone, for the space to be as clear as possible. The plan was that whilst Angus and I went up to Caitir's room, with the kids that were willing to accompany us, the parents would remain downstairs, making sure candles stayed lit and continuing the clean-up operation, making a dent in it, a difference.

Eilidh held my hands before being dropped home by one of the parents. "I'm too old for this," she said, somewhat regretfully. "You need strong, young folk, I don't want to be a hindrance." I remonstrated, but she was insistent. "I'll be doing my part from here, don't you worry. I'm going to sit by the fireside and imagine every one of you bathed in light, and plenty of it. And I won't stop, not until you've all returned."

Together with Angus and me in his car, there was Mr

and Mrs Ludmore and their son Craig, our mood almost buoyant. There's satisfaction in taking action, rather than sitting and waiting for the next attack, we all felt that. It was right what we were doing. It empowered us. I'd even secured Shelley's blessing. In some ways I wished too that she'd been able to come with us. She was such a wise woman, so brave, but I understood where her energies were needed and instead prayed for her safe return via Grey's house.

The drive time whizzed by with no traffic encountered en route, just a steady stream of cars – a convoy – our headlights a blazing trail of defiance.

Parking close to our usual spot, I climbed out of the car, noticing drizzle in the air and a heavy mist starting to swirl.

"The weather's on the change," remarked Angus.

"Let it rain," I said. "Rain is cleansing."

"That's one way of looking at it," Mrs Ludmore commented. "A nice way."

"If that's so," her son quipped, "Skye has to be the cleanest island in the world."

"Not quite," I said, smiling at him. "But soon it will be."

"Good," he answered, serious again. "Because I want things to go back to the way they were, you know with Ally, with all of us."

"They will," Angus ruffled Craig's hair. "Believe it."

That also made me smile, Angus buying into what I'd said, what Shelley had said too. Love. Belief. Forgiveness. I had two in the bag at least.

We convened with the others on the gravel path that led to the lighthouse, our various torches shining, bringing light to where light had been absent for so long.

Looking around I noticed one of our number missing.

"Where's Grant?" I asked.

The silence seemed guilt-ridden for a moment, and then Lainey's mother spoke up. "His parents, they changed their minds, they didn't want him to come."

"Cowards," someone mumbled, but I disagreed.

"If they thought their child might be vulnerable in some way then they're far from that. But those who have come, thank you, thank you so much."

Again there was silence, followed by another comment on the weather.

"Shouldn't be surprised if the rain turns to snow soon, it's so cold."

"Aye, right time of year for it, and if it does, it'll last 'til Christmas and beyond."

I marvelled at that. A white Christmas on Skye, that'd be something to see.

Another parent stamped his feet. It was Ben. "Tell you what, wish I'd bought a flask of whisky too, for medicinal purposes you understand."

Everyone laughed before Mr Ludmore replied, "Let's deal with this first, then there'll be all the time in the world to celebrate."

I hoped so: that life could go back to how it was for these people, as Craig, and as all of them so desperately wanted, with its ups and downs for sure, but nothing extreme, nothing to tip it into the abyss. A steady life, *normality* – it was a gift we often took for granted.

As we made our way to the house, I looked up at the tower, the top of which was lost in cloud, as though a shroud had been thrown over it – a natural occurrence, but I knew it to be something else too: a mockery, a challenge even. I tore my gaze away.

At the door, we waited; every one of us steeling ourselves for what lay beyond. I hoped that by assigning the parents practical tasks, it would keep their hands and minds occupied downstairs, allowing me to address more spiritual matters upstairs without interference. Again, I looked upwards, this time at the window of the bedroom that Caitir had once occupied. Poor, terrified Caitir. What easy prey her father had been, and what terrible consequences it had had for them all.

That's what we refused to be: prey. Not anymore.

"Are you ready?" I said, turning to those gathered beside me.

The response, as ever, was positive.

"Remember what I said earlier, everyone has weaknesses, God knows I do, but we put them aside, we don't take them in there with us. We're here, we're together and we're strong. We can do this. We can restore balance, at the lighthouse and in our lives. We're doing this for Ally and for Moira, for all those who lost their lives here when that ship floundered on the rocks below, and for the Camerons too, who were as much victims as anyone else, especially their children, Caitir and Niall. We're doing it for every one of us."

"When good men do nothing," Angus muttered.

"Sorry?" Diane questioned. "Did you say something?"

"Och, it's just a saying," Angus told her, "a famous one. *The only thing necessary for the triumph of evil is for good men to do nothing.*"

"Oh," Diane said, but unless I was mistaken her eyes seemed to mist, as if she found such a quote incredibly touching. I know I did.

"Amen," said Ben and then began to clap. Slowly the others joined in and I did too. Who were we clapping? Ourselves, I suppose, and why not? Why shouldn't we give ourselves the biggest round of applause ever? These people deserved it.

Bolstered further, we pushed the door open and, single file, trooped inside.

"Keep your torches switched on and light as many tea-lights as possible. At no point let the lights go out completely, that's imperative."

I apologised about the rubbish clearing. "I know it seems a menial task, but it isn't, it heralds change. This is no longer a dumping ground where things that are rotten can thrive. It will soon become a guesthouse, and there are plans for more buildings to be added, so the whole feel of it, the energy, will become more dynamic. It'll attract people, not those looking for cheap thrills, sorry kids, I don't mean any disrespect by that, but it's true. Those who come here in future will be those in search of beauty, who want to immerse themselves in God's Own Country as Angus once called it, and, of course, to enjoy his very own brand of hospitality, which I can highly recommend."

"Aye," Angus said amidst more laughter, "there'll be a roaring log fire, and a good choice of whisky to hand."

"That's right," I said, "keep the home fires burning. Always."

While everyone made themselves busy, Angus, five teenagers instead of six – Craig, Amy, Isabel, Denny and Lainey – and I went upstairs. A total of seven. A good number, I decided, the number of perfection. Perhaps it was providence Grant hadn't come. We all carried torches, back-up torches and had a bagful of tea-lights between us, some of which, even now were being burned downstairs, each tiny flame a protest.

Understandably, the parents were nervous at letting their offspring out of their sight, but at least they weren't far away. I'd already agreed with them to only come running if they heard me shouting the word 'help'. Otherwise, they were to expect some noise, some banging, and crashing, as the conjuring railed against its suppression.

Climbing higher, I was assaulted with a vision – Caitir and Niall and their terrible demise. I expected the assault, but for the subjects to be strangers, not them. It shook me, but quickly I sideswiped the image. Later I'd spend time with their memory, imagining sweet smiles on their faces, their childish wonder at simple things: a favourite meal perhaps, or a walk in the open air. I wasn't like this thing; I wouldn't dwell on the negative.

We reached Caitir's room, it wasn't an attack this time, but I could see her clearly. She was lying on the bed, or at least the residue of her. She was reading a book, trying to lose herself in a story, anything to take her mind off the increasing madness she was being subjected to in her own home. Her parents were arguing below, their voices so loud she could hear every word. In subsequent months, her mother would no longer argue, she'd be afraid to – and the silence that ensued, especially at night, was far worse, because in it you could hear other things: whispers, a sudden peal of laughter, a low scream, none of it from the people inside. Finally, the shade that was Caitir threw the book across the room – frustrated, frightened, and angry too – you couldn't help but be angry here, you fed on it as much as it fed on you. Such a young child and so bewildered, resident in a home that had once been ordinary, but was now filled wall to wall with terror. As for Niall, he barely spoke, barely left his room and no one cared, no one gave a damn.

"Ness, are you okay?"

Angus broke the connection. What I'd seen had taken mere seconds, but the depth of emotion would leave a permanent scar. Her fear and her loneliness, I understood it. There were other children in the room, however, *living* children, I mustn't let the dead consume me. I could help them whereas I couldn't help Caitir. I had to fill my mind with practical tasks too, lest it start to wander again…

"Clear the room," I instructed. "You've each got a bin bag, fill it to the brim."

Torchlight bouncing haphazardly off the walls, we set about our first task. We'd thought to pack latex gloves courtesy of Diane, who worked on reception at a doctor's surgery and had a bundle in her house already. "You never know when they might come in handy," she'd said enigmatically. They were certainly coming in handy now. I don't suppose anyone in the house actually wanted to touch anything that was here, covered as it was in a layer of filth, but there was glass too, some of it broken, and glass could cut.

Whilst we were working diligently, it was Denny who screamed.

"What is it?" I said, straightening up. "What's the matter?"

"Oh nothing." He seemed embarrassed by his actions. "A rat or something."

"A rat?" Lainey sneered. "You sissy."

"It was a big rat!" he retaliated.

"Where's it gone?" asked Craig.

"I hate rats!" declared Isabel.

"Hey, hey, hey," Angus calmed them down. "Think of it as a giant mouse, and mice are cute, aren't they?"

"Well, yeah," Isabel admitted.

"And it's gone now, more scared of us than we are of it."

"Just like the other thing will be," Craig said boldly.

"That's right," I said, encouraging that boldness.

When the room was cleared, I took something else out of the carrier bag we'd brought – salt – and made a large circle with it.

"That's where you sit," I told the group, "inside the circle."

"Because in ritual magic, salt forms a protective circle, one in which summoned energy cannot encroach."

It was Amy who'd recited those words – almost exactly as I'd said them in the hall.

I smiled at the spiritualist in the making. "Whatever happens," I added, "stay inside the circle. In it you'll be safe. If you'd like to take your seats…"

"What about you, Miss, are you sitting in the circle too?"

His somewhat schoolboy address amused me. "Yes, Craig, and so is Angus."

"Good job it's a big salt ring you've drawn then," Angus said, smiling too.

Once seated with our legs crossed in front of us, I suggested we place our torches on the ground. I had one, but the kids and Angus had two, one for each story they were going to tell – and that we hold hands. "Feel the energy that exists between us," I instructed further, "how powerful we are when we stand together. We need to draw on that power, on the positive in each of us, *feed* on it, as this thing has fed on us. You know what, you can feast as much as you like, fill your boots, as long as it's the good stuff. If any negative thoughts creep in, shut the door on them and turn the key."

"It's like witchcraft," giggled Isabel, a little nervously.

"If it is, it's the white variety," I answered. "Remember what I said about the light too, to keep it ever present in your mind, as though it's surrounding us in a bubble."

"And the torches?" asked Amy, more serious than Isabel.

"We turn them off, all except one. Angus, you said you'd tell your ghost story first, so keep yours on. Next up is Craig, then Amy, and so on, remember the rota?"

All nodded.

"When it comes to your turn, switch the first of your torches on, switch the second on when you tell your second story. If either torch should fail, light a tea-light, and if that blows out, light another and another, keep going. There's no shortage, we've plenty with us. That's how we play the game this time, in reverse, instead of lights going off, we keep them coming on. At the end, when they're all fully ablaze, we blast this thing into oblivion."

As torches were turned off, the darkness crept closer, I could hear several sharp intakes of breath, and the hands that were holding mine, tightened their grip.

"Are you ready?"

"We're ready," everyone replied in chorus.

"Then let's begin."

Chapter Twenty-Two

"IT was a wild and stormy night…"

Angus's opening line – the same that he'd used with me when we'd first visited the lighthouse – drew giggles from several of us, including me. That was good, that was what was intended. Laughter was the best kind of energy. To his credit, he didn't falter, but carried on. We'd agreed a maximum of five minutes per story, shorter if possible and I was to oversee, making sure that no one ran over their allotted time, encouraging the next person, watching for subtle changes in behaviour, and dealing with them. We'd also agreed to make each ghost story end on a high note. 'They don't need to be dark, or frightening, they can be heart-warming instead, a spirit is united with the light for example, or gets a message across that he or she hadn't been able to do in life. They might help to solve a mystery. Use your imagination, but use it for the good.' After all, the last thing I wanted was fear to get a stronghold, not when we'd only just managed to kick it to the curb.

Angus's story continued, concerning the ghost of a highwayman parted from his head during an execution, but managing to find it at last, although preferring to carry it under his arm rather than stick it on his neck – the view was better apparently! It was a good story, a classic story –

one that made us all smile because of its familiarity.

Craig was next, his story containing a small amount of gore and more sci-fi than horror, with Artificial Intelligence at its heart, but we could forgive him that. It was thrilling in parts, amusing in others, making us wince only slightly. As soon as he'd uttered the last sentence, he switched his torch on too, chasing away more of the darkness.

Amy's story erred towards the sentimental, centring round a lost child reunited with his mother. As soon as she finished, she switched her torch on – a third light joining the rest.

Isabel told the fourth, Denny the fifth – it was all going so well, and then Lainey started. It was nothing to do with the tale she told, which was harmless enough – it was the energy here, besides ours, fighting back, making her torchlight flicker.

"Damn," she muttered. "I put new batteries in as well."

"Let's just carry on," I said. "Angus, it's your turn again. Limit it to three minutes I think."

He eyed me warily. "Is that necessary?"

"It is."

"Ah, that's a shame, it's a belter this one, but I'll do as you say."

It was another humorous story – this time about the ghost of a cheeky monkey. He had us all in stitches by the end of it, although my laughter was forced. It had grown so much colder in here, the temperature dropping several degrees – had no one else noticed?

When Craig had finished his turn, he picked up the second of his torches and switched that on. It refused to work at all.

"Light a candle," I instructed.

Immediately obeying, he leant across to a selection of tea-lights closest to him, grabbed one of several boxes of matches and lit the flame. It took a few attempts, and a fair bit of swearing as he burnt his fingers, but eventually the candle burst into life, and was a wonderful sight to see – small but perfectly formed. I willed it to stay put, to do its job.

Amy picked up the second of her torches, ready to start her tale, and as she did, she screamed. "Look! There's a spider! Just outside the circle. Oh my God, it's huge! It's close, really close. I can't sit here with that thing next to me."

I looked to where she was pointing and could see nothing but empty space. "Amy, there's no spider."

"There is! There is!"

I sensed panic on the rise, not just in her, but in some of the others too. If I didn't do something, if the spider she thought she was seeing edged closer, she'd bolt, and the others would follow suit. I sighed with exasperation, couldn't help it. A spider – that's all this entity had to do, conjure a spider and the circle would be broken. It was so simple, yet so damned effective; some might even call it genius.

"Amy, look at me. Amy, please. Take your eyes off what you think you can see and look *only* at me."

"I… I…" Despite the preternatural cold, I'd bet she was sweating.

"AMY!" I shouted this time. "Look at me! Every one of you do the same. There is no spider. This thing that we're dealing with, that we're trying to beat, it plays havoc with your imagination, you know that, I've told you that. It'll worm its way into your psyche and it'll dig out your fears, and your phobias, all the stuff that makes you question yourself. Slam the door on it, Amy. Bolt it in place. You have to lock away your fears, just for tonight. There's no way we can break the circle, not until all the lights are shining."

"Is it scared too, Miss?" Craig asked. "Because it knows that we're winning?"

His words were such a relief. "Yes, Craig, it's scared too, very scared. I'm so glad you understand that. We've got Amy's story to go, then Isabel's, Denny's and Lainey's. It's not long now 'til we blast this sucker to kingdom come."

Clearly he approved of my use of language. Turning to Amy, he said, "Listen to her. There's no spider. Get on with your story."

Amy was still rigid, but she relaxed slightly as she moved her gaze from the corner to the centre of the circle again. "It's gone," she said. "It must have crawled off some-where."

"Amy," Angus echoed, "listen to Ness. It was never there."

"But what if it returns?"

"Then… I don't know, I'll try and catch it, although what I'll be grasping at is thin air. Honestly, don't give it another thought. Tell your story, we all want to hear it."

She gave a timid laugh. "It doesn't involve spiders."

"Just as well," Angus said, smiling back at her.

She not only obeyed, she did incredibly well under the circumstances, her voice shaking only slightly here and there as her eyes left mine and roamed elsewhere. When she did this, I had to interrupt. "Look at me, Amy, only me."

Finishing, she picked up the second torch – it came on, but hers, like Lainey's was flickering, growing weaker as she fiddled with it.

"You know what to do," I said. "If it goes out, you light a candle."

She swallowed audibly. "I keep thinking something's crawling on my back," she said, "I know there isn't, but…"

"There really isn't," I said. "We cleared this room, re-member? There were no spiders then and there are none now."

She nodded, but her breathing was heavier too.

"Isabel…" I prompted. "It's your second turn."

"I'm not scared of spiders," she answered.

"Let's not talk about spiders."

"But I don't like rats, or snakes. There won't be any snakes manifesting, will there?"

"Not if you close a door on that fear."

"My story is about monsters though," she continued, "not scary monsters, they're cute actually. They turn out to be the good guys in the end. I based it on *Beauty and the Beast*. This situation, and you, it sort of inspired it."

As flattered as I was, this was no fairy-tale.

"Denny," she said suddenly, "will you stop doing that, shining your light in my eyes?"

"What?" Denny sounded surprised. "I wasn't. I'm point-ing it straight ahead."

"No you weren't, you were shining it at me, blinding me. Turn it away."

"You don't know what you're talking about," Denny continued to object. "I'm not!"

"Denny—"

"Stop!" I commanded. "No arguing. That's one of our

rules, isn't it? We keep calm, we even have a bit of fun, and we shine the lights."

"Some fun this is," whispered one of them, Lainey I think, immediately inciting anger. *How dare she say that! Who does she think she is? Stupid fucking bitch!*

The force of my thoughts shocked me. They made me want to reach out and grab Lainey by the throat, shake her until she was as limp as a rag doll, tear her limbs apart.

"Light another candle," I said, a desperation in my voice that Angus responded to straightway.

"Light a few of them," he added.

We needed the light and I needed to keep calm, close a door on my weakness too – my anger. But it's not easy; it's not bloody easy... "Isabel, please, just tell your story."

She did and it was a good one, as light as I'd hoped, as funny as I'd wished for. Her torch also worked perfectly, and because of that we seemed to settle again.

"Breathe, kids," I reminded them. "Slowly and deeply."

"It's impossible to panic when you breathe like that," Isabel piped up.

"That's the intention," Angus answered for me.

"Denny, yours is the eleventh story," I said. "Almost there. We're almost there."

Denny began his story but he kept faltering... his gaze constantly drawn to another corner of the room, the one behind me. I wanted to look round, to try and see what had captured his attention, but I refrained. If I did, I'd give it validation, and so I kept gently prompting him instead. "Just another minute or so, Denny, and then it's over."

"I... I... Sorry, I can't. I keep forgetting the words."

"Then wrap it up," I suggested. "Any way will do. Give it some kind of ending."

"It's just he keeps laughing at me, that's all."

"No one's laughing at you, Denny."

"There is, it's that man in the corner. He… he… keeps looking at me and laughing."

Denny was a sweet kid, a *brave* kid – he was here after all, when others wouldn't come near – but he was also very overweight with a mop of dark hair that was even more unruly than Angus's. The man he insisted was laughing at him, I think I knew where that was coming from – people *did* laugh at him, his friends, his friends mates, maybe even total strangers. They'd look and they'd laugh at the fat kid. And it hurt. It really hurt. And this thing that was with us, it knew how much its laughter also hurt the boy.

"It's just the seven of us in this room, Denny, that's all."

Denny paused, his expression turning slightly sour. "He's laughing at you too, Miss."

"Then let him," I replied. "I'll tell you what, why don't we laugh along with him, let him know that we find him just as funny."

That horrified Denny. "No, no, please don't do that, it'll make him angry." He hung his head in fear and sadness. "Let's just… ignore him. I can do that, honestly I can."

"He isn't there," I repeated, glancing at Angus who couldn't resist turning his head to see what had transfixed Denny. Having done so, he looked at me and gave a slight shake of the head. A manifestation unique to Denny, as the spider had been for Amy, I only hoped it would fade soon. "Denny, bring the story to an end, then turn on your torch."

He managed to do as I asked, but I could tell he was struggling. His torch came on, but the light was weak.

"Can I light a candle too, Miss?" There was a quiver in his voice.

"Light as many as you want." I was glad to give him something else to focus on.

There was silence again, a few sounds from downstairs managed to pervade, but they sounded so far away, as if at the end of a long, long tunnel. It was isolated on this part of the island, but in this room I felt more isolated still. We all did I think, cut off from the rest of the world, from reality even – playing a game that had serious consequences.

The time for the twelfth story had come – Lainey's second turn. Not all but some torches at least, shone around us, the light confined to the circle that we were sitting in. The candles glowed too, but some had already gone out. No matter, Denny was continuing to light the ones he could, pushing those that remained lit away from him, making room for more. There was an obsessive quality to his behaviour, and the others, plus Angus, noticed. The game had to come to a head soon – one way or another.

"Lainey, can you please take your turn?"

The girl tore her gaze from Denny to stare at me. Was I mistaken or had her expression changed? There wasn't fear in it, or worry, not any more. She looked… *amused*.

"Lainey, are you okay?"

"I'm fine," she insisted.

"Keep your story short, two or three minutes is fine, then Angus can finish the game. The light is so much stronger than the dark, and we are so much stronger if we work together. And that's what we're doing; we've got each other's backs. I'm proud of you, Lainey, I'm so damned proud. I'm proud of all of you. What a great team we are."

Her expression was beginning to return to normal, just

as another torch went out.

"I'm scared." It was Amy, her eyes darting furiously around again.

"I know you are–" I began, but Angus interrupted me.

"Amy, Lainey, all of you, we fight this thing or it wins. We've come so far, do you really want to give up now?"

"Lainey, come on," urged Craig.

"Okay, okay," she responded, no hint of amusement in her voice at least, she sounded defiant instead – whether that was in our favour or not, I couldn't tell.

Taking a deep breath, looking at each of us in turn, her gaze finally came to rest on me. In the glare of the torch-light, with the darkness at her back, she *had* altered. She seemed bigger than she was before, and she had a yellowish cast to her eyes. Was it because of the flames spluttering at her feet? Not a cheerful yellow, it was dirty instead…

As she opened her mouth, I braced myself.

"Once upon a time there was a girl, a lonely girl, a girl who was misunderstood."

Don't rise to it, I told myself. *This may have nothing to do with you.*

"She had hair as dark as mine, and lived in a big house with her mummy and daddy, and her brothers and sisters."

The skin on the back of my neck began to tingle.

"Her bedroom was tiny, the smallest of all the bed-rooms, but in it she would hide from the world. And not just the world, but those who were from other worlds too."

Should I interrupt? I couldn't, the twelfth story had to be told. It would be all right if I just didn't take the bait.

"One of those that she hid from was her twin, her *dead* twin. Even though the twin was nice to her, *needed* her, this girl wasn't nice back, she was mean to her poor dead twin, nasty, and she was that way because she'd learnt to be. Her mother had taught her well."

I couldn't do it, just sit there and listen, I tried, but words tumbled out of my mouth. "Lainey, if you don't feel well, if something's wrong—"

"Let me speak!" she hissed and not only me, all of us flinched. Reminding myself that this was someone's child, not something terrible, I tried again to reach her.

"Lainey—"

"Oh this mother of hers, she taught her hatred, anger and fear, and all of this the girl practised on her twin, someone who'd suffered enough, who was dead for Christ's sake! She'd killed her in the womb; sucked the life from her. That's why her mother felt the way she did, that's the true reason. Her mother knew the twin that lived was evil."

"STOP IT!" I shouted. "STOP IT NOW, LAINEY!"

As Angus looked at me in both shock and bewilderment, as the teenagers looked at me in that way too, Lainey began to snarl. "The twin that lived then decided to hurt her family more, to bring great shame on them and herself. She hurt her twin too, the twin who'd always tried to help her, to comfort her, the twin who'd forgiven her for the life that she'd stolen. But the living twin couldn't forgive, her soul was black, and her heart was twisted."

"Lainey…" My voice seemed to have lost its strength as sobs threatened to choke me.

"Go on, Ness, tell them what you did, to your twin, to your family, and to yourself. Tell them about the madness that runs thick in your veins…"

"I'm not mad," I denied as the lights flickered, but again my voice was weak.

"The psychiatrists said you were."

"I'd been *driven* mad," I countered, so many shocked pairs of eyes on me, "but it was only temporarily. I swear I'm *not* mad."

"You are," Lainey insisted, "and yet here we sit, listening to you." She shrugged. "Perhaps we're mad too."

"Ness... Lainey..." Angus didn't know which one of us to address first.

"Tell us what you did," Lainey took no notice of him at all, her gaze, that filthy yellow gaze, fixed solely on me, "when you were thirteen."

"No," my voice was a mere whisper, "I can't." I was drenched in shame all over again. Why couldn't I close the door on what had happened, why had I never been able to do that? How ironic, that of all of us here, I was the weakest link. "We need to end this game."

"We can't," Lainey replied, "not until the thirteenth ghost story's been told. And it's your turn, Ness. It's your story that completes the game."

Chapter Twenty-Three

1975

HAPPY thirteenth birthday!

The card I held in my hand, the cheery greeting printed in large red letters against a backdrop of a girl on a scooter, felt flimsy. The words, the girl, equally as cheery, seemed to mock me. Happy was the very opposite of what I was feeling as I sat at the table in our dining room, my brothers and sisters around me, chatting with each other, but rarely with me – even though this was all supposedly in my honour. Dad was trying at least. At the head of the table, he smiled in my direction, even raised his eyebrows a couple of times as if issuing some sort of apology. As for Mum, she was in the kitchen – spending as much time as possible in there, an avoidance tactic. I knew it, and so did everyone else.

Since the miscarriage last year she'd been even more distant with me. Whenever I did catch her glancing my way, the look in her eyes was almost more than I could bear. I'd stopped looking lately, stopped seeking any kind of acceptance. I wasn't as young, as naive, or as hopeful as I used to be, I knew when I was on a highway to nowhere.

As I sat there, toying with my birthday meal –

hamburger and chips, my favourite, or at least it used to be, nothing seemed to taste good lately – I furtively glanced around the room. It wasn't just my birthday, it was hers too – my twin's. She hadn't shown herself since this morning, when she'd dragged me from sleep, excited about the day ahead.

We're thirteen! We're thirteen!

She kept saying it, over and over again, the shape of her more substantial than it had ever been. Her hair, her clothes, the heart shape of her face, it was all mine, but my eyes, I swear they were emptier than hers.

I'd had to go to school – no day off for the birthday girl, not if my mother could help it. The teacher had made a bit of fuss over me, got the other kids to sing *Happy Birthday,* but few, if any, had done so with enthusiasm. I wanted them to stop. I wanted to get to my feet and yell at them to shut up. So what if it *was* my birthday? But I sat there and endured it, my hands clasped under my desk, my nails digging deep into the palm of my hands.

And then the bell had rung and I walked home alone, to this: a birthday tea, a family gathering, the only presents given to me 'serviceable' ones: a flannelette nightdress to replace my old one, socks, a winter scarf, and vests. Nothing frivolous, nothing fun, no make-up, not even a new book – how I'd wished for another Brontë book, *Wuthering Heights* this time. Perhaps they'd have it in the library, I could always borrow it from there.

Having finished their meal, two of my sisters started complaining.

"Where's Mum? Me and Suzy want to go out tonight, we can't hang around for long."

"And I've got homework," said Paul, "I need to get on

with it really."

They were itching to leave the dining table. Dad too, he kept glancing at his watch and then at the TV – clearly worried about missing something, the news probably.

"Love," he called through to the kitchen. "How long will you be?"

"Not long," came the irritated reply. "Just give me a minute, will you?"

To do what, I thought? Brace yourself to face me again, your demon daughter.

Eventually she left the kitchen and entered the room, a cake in her hands, one that, to my amazement, looked homemade. I'd *never* had a homemade cake before.

"Get the lights!" my father said, nodding at Ollie. "Quick!"

In the darkness, the cake, with its white icing and jammy middle was remarkably pretty, with not just one or two candles, but thirteen, blazing merrily away.

A voice interrupted my wonder. *Ness, look at our cake!*

It's my cake. Straightaway, I shot the thought back. *Just mine!*

But Ness, it's our birthday, both of us.

That cake is mine!

As the second chorus of *Happy Birthday* began, I tried to ignore just how mean I was being, didn't truly understand the reason why – my moods had been up and down a lot lately, more down than up if I'm honest. Maybe it was the number of candles that did it. As far as I could remember there'd only ever been two or three in the past, and not just on my cake, but all my siblings' cakes. 'Candles are an unnecessary expense,' Mum would say, if someone happened to complain. 'We're not made of money.' But today I'd got the correct number *and* a cake she'd baked herself, not something shop bought. She'd made an effort – a *huge* effort – and my eyes watered to see it. Perhaps I wasn't so hardened after all; perhaps I did care. And wonder of wonders, perhaps she did as well.

As the cake was set before me, I leant forward to blow the candles out.

Let's blow them out together.

Still my twin was insisting. Forgetting myself, I turned my head to the side and glared at her. *No!*

"Ness," my mother's voice contained its usual curtness. "Will you hurry up? I don't want wax dripping all over that cake."

"Sorry," I muttered, chancing a smile at her. She didn't return the gesture.

Drawing in another deep breath, I warned my twin again. *Just stay back.*

Maybe it was this way even when you had a living twin. Sometimes, just sometimes, you wanted your own space, a bit of individuality, and a fuss made of you and you alone.

As I went to exhale, she beat me to it – the candles spluttered for a moment, as if on my side, as if protesting, but finally giving in. I stood there, staring at the extinguished candles, at the smoke trails, stunned. How was she able to do that? She'd already used a fair amount of energy this morning, materialising to such an extent. She'd need time to recharge before interacting on this scale, a day or two, a week – not mere hours.

Something inside me – brittle for so long – snapped. Without thinking of the consequences, I lunged forward, one hand connecting with the cake and swiping it off the table, knocking it flying across the room, all the while screaming in my head, *NO! NO! NO!*

It wasn't just in my head I realised, I was screaming out loud too, and not just those words but far more. "You're always here, you're always interfering. I don't want you anymore, don't you realise? I want you to leave me alone. You didn't have a birthday. Not really. Only I did. This is *my* birthday, and *my* cake, and those were *my* candles."

Too late, I realised the horror on the faces that surrounded me, my twin's included. And then as always, from those who were living anyway, came the suppressed humour, the tired sighs, the eye rolling, and my mother's terrible ire.

"Look what you've done!" she screamed. "You... You... I don't know what you are!" There seemed to be genuine confusion in that last cry. My mother honestly didn't know what she'd spawned. "That's it, your birthday's over. Go to your room. Get out of my sight!"

In just as much shock as she was, I forced my legs to move, my feet connecting with the goo of the cake that lay splattered on the floor, slipping and sliding momentarily, causing even more merriment amongst some of my siblings. Once in my room, as much a sanctuary for me as the kitchen had been for my mother, I slammed the door shut, threw myself on my bed and prepared for the sobs that would surely wrack my body. It surprised me when they didn't come, when my eyes remained stubbornly dry.

Pushing myself up, I shunted along to the edge of my bed and sat there instead. How long for I don't know. Time had ground to a halt. Eventually I could hear activity on the landing – my brothers and sisters, my parents, preparing for bed, passing my room but not bothering to call out to the occupant inside. Silence descended. My twin was close by, I could feel her, but she had the good sense to keep her distance.

At some point I rose from my bed with the intention of going downstairs to the kitchen. Before I did, however, I walked across to the mirror that hung on the far wall and stared at my reflection. I hated what I saw – the monster that faced me.

Gently easing open the bedroom door, managing to avoid all the creaking floorboards, I padded downstairs, carpeted floor soon giving way to cold tiles. In the kitchen, I didn't bother to turn the light on. The darkness suited my purpose. I welcomed it, wondering just how dark it was going to get; not on this side, the other side – the darkness in which things existed.

Ness, don't.

Finally, my twin had dared to materialise, but I ignored her. Instead, I reached for the wooden block just behind the toaster and chose what I hoped was the sharpest knife.

I'm sorry. It was mean of me to blow out the candles, you're right, but I couldn't help myself.

Calmly I turned towards her – not substantial, not anymore, she was barely a shade.

"That's because you're a monster too," I said.

She seemed to fade a little more at that.

The knife in my hand, I stared at the blade, not gleaming, not in the darkness, but dull.

If you do that, I'll tell Mum. I'll race upstairs and tell her.

I shrugged. "She can't see you."

You know that she can.

"She'll never admit it. Besides," I lifted my head to stare at her again, "I thought you'd be glad. I'll be dead like you soon."

She shook her head – a fractured gesture. *I want you to live, for both of us.*

I think I actually snarled as I lifted my left arm, palm side up.

I'll tell Mum! Her voice was a screech that rattled inside my head.

"Tell her," I said, "and tell her this if she's listening, she's a monster too, and I will never forgive her for denying what I am, when she's the one I must have inherited it from. And there's something else – I blame you just as much. Both of you have driven me to this."

Were those sobbing sounds she was making? My dead twin reduced to tears? If she expected sympathy, she'd be disappointed. I had nothing more to give.

Ness, I love you. I've always loved you.

The knife biting into my flesh, I felt no pain, it was as though I'd gone completely numb. Leaning forward slightly, my face close to hers, I whispered more words – her sobs becoming wails on hearing them, on seeing the knife turn crimson.

Chapter Twenty-Four

AS I finished my story, I raised my head to find several pairs of eyes staring back at me. I'd never talked about what had happened to me at thirteen. For twelve years, I'd kept the shame of it locked inside, burning, always burning. Obviously, I hadn't bled out. My mother had found me, my father dialled for an ambulance, doing their duty, as parents should. I'd never talked about the aftermath either – the psychiatric care I'd received – *enforced* care – the lies I'd had to tell in order to escape its clutches: 'No, I can't see spirits. Yes, I made it all up.' Was it to seek attention, they'd asked? After all, I came from a big family, trying to get noticed must be hard at times. I'd nodded at that, 'Yes, it was all to seek attention.'

Such answers kept the doctors satisfied.

"Miss?" It was Craig with his typical schoolboy address. "What happened to your twin? Have you seen her since?"

It was my twin who'd captured his imagination, not the way my family had treated me, or my suicide attempt. Somehow there was comfort in that.

"Miss?"

"No," I replied, "I haven't seen her."

Another voice piped up: Isabel's. "What happens now?"

Now? Angus's gaze was questioning too.

"Erm..."

"Miss." Not Craig, it was Lainey, her eyes had returned to normal, but something in her voice unnerved me still. "You haven't turned on your torch."

"My torch?" I looked down at what lay in my hands, at the slim metal casing – the torch! How had I forgotten it? It was the whole point of the game!

"And your story," Lainey continued with a sneer, "it wasn't exactly uplifting, was it?"

"Just switch on the torch, Ness," Angus instructed.

I did my utmost to obey, but my hands had started to shake.

"It's cold in here, Miss, really cold," Craig said.

"I know, I know," I said. Where was the bloody switch?

"Ness, give it to me." Still Angus sounded calm

"Haven't you noticed how cold it is?" I whispered to him. "Surely you've noticed?"

"Give me the torch."

"No, it has to be me who switches it on, it has to be."

There! My fingers had found the switch. I pressed down. Nothing happened. I pressed again. Still it refused to comply. I jabbed and jabbed, but no matter how hard I tried, there was no thirteenth light. Damn it, it had to come on. It had to! I *willed* it to come on.

"MISS!"

It was Craig, screaming as all the lights went out, just as they'd done on my thirteenth birthday, all the torches and all the candles, plunging us into darkness so intensely that for a moment I doubted my own existence within it. *What you can't see...* But I *did* exist, as did the thing that resided in such darkness – it was here in this room, still intent on playing.

The scrape of boots on the floor indicated that people

were scattering.

"Don't break the circle!" I shouted, but it was in vain. With no protection, and no light, the darkness was winning. Amy's cries confirmed that.

"The spider! It's back. It's on me, I can feel it." So fast she'd descended into panic, providing fuel for the fire. "There's more than one, there's loads of them. They're huge!"

I shouted for Angus. "Will you see to her?"

"Aye, leave it to me. Amy, where are you? Where the hell are you?"

It wasn't a large room, so he should have no problem in finding her, she should be at arm's length. Except she wasn't. No one was. The room had become vast, a cavern, one that was filled with more cries and more screams. "Miss! Miss! Where are you?"

"Craig, I'm here. Make your way to the door!"

"I don't know where the door is!"

"It's… It's…" He was right, where was it? I spun round and round, completely disorientated.

"Stop shining that light in my eyes!" It was Isabel, scolding Denny.

"Isabel," I shouted, "Denny's not doing anything. There *is* no light, remember?"

"He is, he's blinding me," she continued, and then her voice faltered, became more wary. "But… it's a strange kind of light, it's… it's… *dirty*."

"Isabel, where are you?" I shouted.

"I'm here. Where are you? I can't see anything, because of Denny, because of this… horrible, horrible light. DENNY, WILL YOU STOP IT!"

She began to cry, and at that moment Denny screamed

too. "That man, the one laughing at me, he's coming over. Look! He's as clear as anything. He's going to get me!"

"There's no man, Denny," I answered. "Shut your eyes if that helps, but he's honestly not there. Angus, Angus, where are you?"

Gradually, I became aware of other voices, those belonging to the terrified parents gathered at the door to Caitir's room, a door that was so far away, in another time, another realm almost. I hadn't called for backup, or yelled out 'help', but we needed them and the light that they could bring more than ever. We needed to up our game, not panic further.

"Ben, Mrs Ludmore," I responded, striding across the room to where I thought the door might be. I took so many strides, an impossible amount given the room's size. I tried shouting too, wondering if my voice might sound as far away as theirs, if they'd be able to hear me at all. "All of you, force the door open if you can. We can't seem to find it and all the lights have gone out. We need you in here. We need you now!"

"You're not going anywhere." It was Lainey. In the darkness she'd found me, her voice with that strange slithering quality, her eyes the only thing visible... and yellow.

"You don't frighten me," I said, straightening my spine and preparing for battle.

"Filthy bitch," she continued, as if she hadn't heard my forced words of bravado. "What a burden you were for your family to carry. Such shame you brought on them."

I swallowed and the cries around me – all of them – began to fade, even Isabel's shrill insistence that there were snakes in the room now as well as spiders, as she began to retch with horror. "I've confessed to that shame," I said, "right here in this room, in front of all of you. It's no secret anymore."

The thing that was Lainey but wasn't, that was *masquerading* as Lainey, pushed its face into mine. "You think that words absolve you?"

I stood my ground "Why shouldn't they? Words are powerful."

"You feel cleansed?"

In a way I did, of that sin at least. A secret that's been told loses its power.

It picked up on my thoughts.

"But what about the other words you said?"

"The other words?" *Don't think about it, Ness. Don't let it trick you.*

"The worst words. You haven't confessed to them yet have you?"

"Get out of my way. I'm going to find the door."

She laughed – a hateful sound. "There's no escape from here."

"There's always a way out."

"That's just it, sometimes there isn't."

As I stared at her, Lainey grew more visible, the darkness around her seeming to shrink back. A girl of average height, she was becoming smaller, withered almost… and familiar too. Opening her mouth, she began to speak – her voice so much like mine.

"Why'd you do it? I said I was sorry."

I tried to retreat, to turn even, but I was rigid, my feet glued to the floorboards. Around me, all sounds had faded entirely. There was just me in the room… me and my twin.

"Y…you're not her," I stuttered. "You're pretending to

be."

"You're denying what you see?"

"You're. Not. Her." It couldn't be, not this withered, shrivelled thing, this husk.

"After what you said, Ness, a husk is what I became."

Wildly, I shook my head. "I won't be fooled."

"I told you I was scared of the dark, didn't I? I told you that there were things in it… *waiting*. Bad things, evil, vampiric. I told you all of that and still you banished me."

I lifted my hand and rubbed at my eyes. "No… This isn't… I didn't…"

"YOU DID! YOU BANISHED ME!"

"I… Because…"

"And all because of something I did when I was a child."

"You're not real!"

"I'm your twin, I'm part of you."

"You're dead."

"Because you sucked the life from me, and then you left me in the dark to fend for myself. Mum was right about you all along. You're the demon that walks amongst us."

Tears! Damn them for falling, but they were, gushing from my eyes as blood had once gushed from my wrists. What she'd done, my birthday cake, it had been the final straw, but she was right, we *were* kids, both of us – only thirteen. *Ness, I love you. I've always loved you.* Those were her last words to me. But my last words to her… what had they been?

"I never want to see you again, not even in death." Lainey – no, my twin – was repeating them pitch perfect. "If you break that rule, if you try and contact me, if you plead, if you cry, even if you beg, I will ignore you. I will never, *ever* acknowledge you again. That's what you said,

Ness. To me, the one who loved you. The only one who ever loved you!"

And I'd hated her for that too. I'd blamed her for all those that didn't.

I couldn't stand it any longer, the weight of all that hate too heavy to bear. As I fell to my knees, the husk became the victor.

"That's right." There was another voice in my ear. Again it was familiar. "We've won."

It was Mum, gloating. Whether she was a conjuring or not didn't matter – she was here, in my head. She was *always* in my head.

Ness! Ness! My twin's voice had changed – it wasn't as scathing as before. Despite that, I didn't look up, didn't want to see again what she'd become, because of me.

Ness! Look at me. Please!

"Stay on your knees, girl." It was Mum again. "It's where you belong, in the gutter, crawling alongside other vile things. A witch, a mad witch. We should have let you bleed."

Ness, quick! You have to be quick! Ness, listen to me. Look at me.

How I wanted to curl in a ball, and go quietly mad once more. My head was pounding, my heart beating as frantically as the wings of a caged bird. When was enough enough? Why wouldn't my heart just stop? Release, Shelley had called it. If I had a knife…

You knew. I aimed the words at my mother but only in thought. *You kept saying I was a liar, over and over, and yet you knew. That's why I didn't bleed out, why you found me so quickly that night, because she did what she'd said she'd do. She saved me.*

My twin.

Ness!

Still she was calling.

Please!

I couldn't lift my head; all strength had deserted me.

"Ness!"

Go away.

"Ness!"

"Just go away," I repeated, able to speak out loud this time.

"Go away? Are you joking? I'm not going anywhere. It's taken me ages to find you in the first place. I thought I never would. Come on, soldier, up you get, on your feet."

Strong hands lifted me. Was this a trick again, another act of cruelty?

"Angus?" I said. "Is it you?"

"Who else?" he said, and I remembered his cheeky grin, his eyes always so enlivened. What would this do to him, this experience at the lighthouse? How would it taint him?

"Oh, Angus." How many tears could I cry this night? There was a reservoir inside me whose dam had burst. "I was wrong. I'm so sorry. We've lost the game."

"Lost? I don't think so."

Barely registering his denial, I rushed onwards. "I've put you in danger, all of you. I was mad to bring you all back here. I *am* mad. Officially. You know that now."

"You're a little quirky at times, I'll admit. But... I kind of like that in a girl."

"Angus!" I shouted. "Listen to me!"

It was what my twin had shouted – mere seconds before – and I'd ignored her. Would he do the same?

It seemed not. Grabbing my face between his hands, he

brought it closer to his.

"We haven't lost. I found you, in this… whatever this is. It didn't want us to find each other, I know it didn't, but we did anyway, thank Christ! Isn't that some kind of triumph?"

A triumph? We were standing in this wretched room, on a remote spot on a remote island, at the mercy of something terrible, something evil, and he was talking about triumphs? I was about to retaliate, to try again to get him to listen to me, to beat against his chest if that's what it took, my fists pummelling, as the fury inside sought release too, but then I stopped. This thing *had* tried to separate us; we're all so much easier to attack that way. Standing here, with Angus, I still felt scared, ashamed and angry. Such strong emotions couldn't disappear in an instant, but one thing I didn't feel was vulnerable, not anymore, not with him by my side. Perhaps he was right. It was a triumph after all.

"Angus…" I began, but he silenced me, bringing me closer to him and placing his lips on mine – *kissing* me.

As he did, light flooded the room – not just the dim glow of tea-lights, of torches, all of them struggling. It was a massive flood of light, blinding in its intensity.

Angus pulled away.

"What the…?" I said. Had we died? That thought honestly crossed my mind.

I could see Angus's face clearly, his *smiling* face.

"Good old Ron," he said. "He must have asked for Liam's help after all."

Chapter Twenty-Five

"LIAM'S here?" I quizzed. Around me, I could see the others – Craig, Amy, Isabel, Denny and Lainey – and they were looking as bewildered as I'm sure I was. Lainey in particular, kept staring at the light and blinking, recovering with every passing second.

Angus nodded in reply. "He is. And just in the nick of time if you ask me."

"The light, where's it coming from?"

"Where'd you think it's coming from?"

"I..."

His eyes widened with amusement. "It's not a heavenly light, if that's what you're thinking, although... in a way perhaps it is."

Like Lainey I blinked. It was the closest thing to a heavenly light I'd ever seen.

The door swung wide, the parents almost falling over themselves with the effort of getting it to open. Looking wildly around, they quickly located their various offspring, running to them and enfolding them in their arms just as they'd done before the event.

"Thank God you're all right," I heard Diane say to Lainey.

"I... I think I'm all right," she replied.

"What happened?" her mother continued. "There was so much noise and commotion coming from in here, we raced up the stairs, but the door was stuck. We tried so hard to get it open, but it wouldn't budge. Can you believe it? An old door like that? We were going frantic out there, all of us. It was awful, we felt so helpless. Oh, Lainey," she cried, throwing her arms around her daughter again. "I'm so relieved you're okay. We wouldn't have given up; we would have broken that damned door down to get in. No devil's going to keep me from my child." The outpouring of emotion over, she started to squint. "Where *is* that light coming from? Not the tower, surely? The lens hasn't worked in years."

Before anyone could approach me, I made for the door too, leaving the room in as much of a hurry as they'd entered it.

"What you doing? Where you going?" Angus fell into step beside me.

"To the tower," I said. "I need to be as close to the source of the light as possible."

"Why?"

Before heading down the staircase, I stopped briefly to answer him, noting the baffled look on his face. "For good reasons, Angus, *personal* reasons. You said Liam is here. How come? When we spoke to Ron, he specifically said he didn't want us to involve him."

"Aye, but I spoke to Ron again."

"When?"

"His was the phone call after Shelley. I explained what had happened to Ally, and then I left it with him to decide what to do for the best. I... erm... I trowelled it on thick."

I couldn't help but smile at that. "Trowelled it on thick?

As if there was a need for that."

"Aye, well, you know how the saying goes, things could always be worse. His conscience must have got the better of him, and he decided to contact Liam after all. It's a fair drive from Carlisle to Skye, but Liam, God bless him, obviously made it. No one else around here knows how to operate the lens." He cocked his head to the side, his face youthful, but his eyes wise. "I thought it'd help, you know, it being the mother of all lights."

"It's not quite," I said, "but thank you. It does help. It helps a lot. Thanks for the kiss too."

He reared back slightly, a big grin on his face. "I don't think I've ever been formally thanked for kissing someone before."

"It's like you said, I'm quirky."

"That you are, Ness, that you are."

As touching as this exchange was, the night wasn't over – not yet. Whatever was here was still at my heels.

With Angus following, I flew down the stairs faster than I'd ever done before. Below, the living room was largely clear of the debris that had carpeted it – the parents had done a great job. Barely any candles remained lit, but those that were flickered valiantly, as impressive in their own way as anything bigger. Making my way to the front door, I pulled it open and stared outwards – the rain had turned to sleet, the clouds as low as ever. The wind was picking up too, and blowing my hair across my face.

"Where's the service room?" I asked Angus.

"It's beside the tower, follow me."

With the gravel beneath our feet, we did as we'd done so often these last few days; we put our heads down and forged ahead. Sure enough, in a small room to the side of the tower, one that had had its door wrecked, probably years before, stood Ron McCarron and a man younger than him but who shared the same stocky build.

"Ron!" I had to shout over the wind. "Thank you, thank you so much. And you're Liam?"

"Aye, I am," the younger man shouted back. "I hope we've been able to help. We went to Angus's house first, and it was Eilidh who told us that you'd all come here." He glanced in the direction of the light that blazed. "I didn't think I had a hope of getting the stand-by generator to work, not after all this time. This salty air, it rusts stuff to buggery. But between Dad and me we managed it. We only bloody managed it!" He laughed. "Don't ask me how though, I don't know, but it wasn't as hard as I thought. In fact," he stopped laughing and looked genuinely perplexed, "it wasn't hard at all. It shouldn't even be possible. Anyway, it's a light! It's static though, it won't sweep. I hope that's okay?"

"Okay? It's brilliant, in every sense of the word. How did you know we needed it?"

He shrugged, a grin as wide as any that Angus could muster on his face. "How?"

I nodded.

"What else are you supposed to fight the forces of darkness with?"

I think it's safe to say I'm not particularly demonstrative, I've never been encouraged in that respect, but I practically threw myself into Liam's arms. "Thank you, thank you so much." Extricating myself from him I then hugged Ron. "You're a good man," I said.

"And you're a good lass," he returned. "We both have demons to fight, but we can do it. We're capable."

"We just have to believe it?"

"Aye, it's as hard and as simple as that."

"It's what we make it, I suppose."

He nodded. "It is. Now away, lass, get on with whatever it is you have to do. We have no idea if and when the generator will fail. Like Liam said, it shouldn't have worked at all."

I did as he instructed, leaving the service room and drawing closer to the tower as lightning pierced the clouds. I looked upwards. *Oh no, you don't, the elements are on our side, not yours.* I was no expert at Reiki, I've mentioned that, but, making the symbol for *Cho Ku Rei* again, I mentally called on Earth, Wind, Air and Fire to assist us and us alone – utilising natural elements for natural purposes only. Certainly, if Shelley had done what she'd promised to do, one of those elements – fire – was right now engulfing Grey's former home, breaking the chain, as she put it. Keeping the Reiki mantra at the forefront of my mind, I carried on walking – deep rolling thunder accompanying me.

Angus was once more by my side, but at the door to the tower I stopped him.

"I have to do this alone," I said.

Worry darkened his features. "But what if you need me?"

"Angus, I *do* need you, I couldn't have done any of this without you, but it's as I said, this next step is personal."

His eyes flickered towards the main building. "It's not a good idea to go up there alone."

"Because I'm weak?" I said, understanding his gesture.

He started to object, but I held up my hand, not quite finished.

"Not all the time, I'm not saying that, but on occasions I *am* weak. I let negativity swamp me. I don't have the strength to fight it all the time, and maybe I never will. But that's because I'm human, I'm flawed, and sometimes I can only take so much."

Reaching out, he took my hands, his thumbs pushing back the sleeves of the coat I wore. I knew what he wanted: to see for himself the damage I'd once inflicted.

"There's strength in admitting that," he said, his thumbs gently rubbing the scarred tissue. "Great strength." Dragging his gaze from my wrists, he stared into my eyes. "I'll be here when you've finished whatever it is you have to do up there. I'll be waiting."

Knowing that, lent me strength too.

* * *

I took the cast iron stairs two at a time in places, more thunder drowning out the clatter of my shoes against the treads that spiralled upwards.

It wasn't a tall tower, but I was breathless by the time I reached the top. To access the outside gallery, I pushed open an iron door, praying that it wasn't rusted and would give way. I was so relieved when it did. Poking my head through, I was instantly hit by a blast of air; sleet coating my cheeks, to lie frozen there. Quickly, I had to shield my eyes. Being so close to source could cause permanent damage; my daring might cost me like it did Icarus from Greek mythology, but I wouldn't stay for long, just until, as Ron had said, I'd done what I needed to do.

Still hardly daring to open my eyes, I eased out onto the gallery. The exposed balcony ran all the way around the underside of the lantern room, which itself was enclosed by glass windows, storm panes I think they're called, able to withstand 'the fine Scottish weather' as Eilidh once termed it. The railing was at waist height and I had to grab hold of it in order to steady myself, for the wind was capable of knocking me off my feet, which might send me plummeting below.

Madness, that's what this was, sheer madness to be up here when the lens was on, in the midst of a storm. But so what? I'd been mad before. Rather than fear it, I'd embrace the extreme weather, the curious mixture of heat from the lens and cold from the air somehow managing to negate each other. I'd throw my head back in the wind, I'd listen as the sea smashed against the rocks, imagining the blue men, the storm kelpies, watching and waiting. I'd marvel too as the lightning kept chasing the darkness. And I'd roar – louder than a lion.

Taking a deep breath, I opened my mouth as wide as I could and, with one giant exhalation I screamed for all the hurt and the agony I'd ever endured; for all the sorrow, the blame and the guilt that had marked me from the day I'd come into this world kicking and crying; for the baby born just minutes after me who'd never cried at all. I screamed for all the hurt that I'd caused, the blame that I'd so wrongly apportioned; for my immaturity, my jealousies, my pettiness, my refusal to accept love when love was offered; for my insistence on embracing hatred instead, and becoming something hateful too. I screamed because of my gift that so often seemed like a curse, it was such a burden to bear. I screamed for my desire to be normal when normal I'd never be. I screamed at injustice and prejudice; for those who felt the need to hit out at what they couldn't understand; for my mother's denial and the loathing in her eyes whenever she looked at me; for the weakness in my father, and the indifference of my brothers and sisters. I howled at the psychiatrists who only ever believed me when I lied. I cried for what I'd done, not just to myself, but also to my twin; for being her shadow side, the darkness to her light; for the irony of that. And I screamed because of how weak I was... still. I might crave forgiveness from my twin, but I couldn't dredge up forgiveness for my mother, not after all that she'd done. There was strength in honesty – Angus had said that. Was it true? Could it really be true?

My voice hoarse, I continued to scream, to let go what I could, to accept what I couldn't, the expulsion as dark as anything we'd encountered in Caitir's bedroom, joining forces with it no doubt, as like called to like. With my back to the lens I stared into the abyss and remembered what she'd said: *My dark isn't like your dark. There are things in it.*

"I'm sorry," I shouted, my raw throat not the only thing responsible for the cracking of my voice, "for all of it. The husk that was pretending to be you in Caitir's room, its voice changed, right at the end. Was that you then? Truly you? You asked me to look, to listen, and to be quick about it. I didn't realise... It's only just occurred to me that it was the real you. I ignored you, but I didn't mean to, not that time. Are you here? Are you anywhere?"

As my eyes strained to see, I could tell she'd been right; there *were* things in the darkness. I could see them, so many things, innumerable, twisting and writhing, agonised things that wanted to crawl towards me, and drag me into the darkness with them, but they couldn't. The light that I was at the centre of was just too bright. It would obliterate them if they dared, as I had dared – like Grey's house, like Icarus, they'd burn too. One other thing, one *important* thing: they couldn't hurt me any more than I'd been hurt already. *That's* why I was the person for the job, and why Shelley had wished I wasn't.

The things – it wasn't my place to name them – retreated. Not far, never far, but far enough. As long as there was light at the lighthouse, and a lightness of being too, they'd keep their distance.

As I continued to stare, I was grateful: there was no mirror image staring back at me. My twin wasn't part of it.

Chapter Twenty-Six

FROM rain to sleet to snow, there was a heavy and glorious swathe. As awed as I was by what was this time a natural phenomenon, brightening the night further, the people around me took it in their stride, as they took so much. Slowly but steadily we all left Minch Point and made our way back to our respective homes, the lighthouse still miraculously blazing behind us; a beacon in the night, an attraction, for all that was right.

Later, when we were ensconced in Eilidh's living room, with endless cups of tea on the go, and a bottle of Talisker too, Angus wanted to know if the darkness had gone forever.

"It's always there," I explained, "in some propensity, but give it nothing to feed on and its strength will continue to deplete."

"This is good news for your Uncle Glenn too, Angus," Eilidh said. "He'll be pleased."

"Are you looking forward to taking over?" I asked and he nodded. "You'll make a brilliant manager," I added. "There's no doubt about it, you're the man for the job."

"Will you come and visit when it's up and running as a guesthouse?" I picked up the plea in his voice, as did Eilidh, who lowered her eyes to stare at her hands.

"Of course I will," I answered. "In time."

We'd both have to be content with that.

The snow prevented any thoughts of an immediate departure and so I stayed for a few more days, just relaxing, doing nothing more than that, enjoying short walks with Angus in the snow, even having a snowball fight – several of them, collapsing in a heap of giggles at the end of every one. I was finally allowing myself to play, but, oh, how I missed the one who'd wanted to play first. We'd also rung Raigmore to find out about Ally. She'd much improved, according to her mother, who came to the phone to speak to us.

"She's like a different girl. It's in her face, you know, it's more relaxed, her skin not as taut. She even smiled today, the old smile, the one that lights up her eyes. Ben told me what you did at the lighthouse, what you all did. Is it over? Please tell me it's over."

I assured her it was, and stressed the importance of keeping Ally's world calm, ordered and familiar in the coming months, as she'd need time to recover completely.

"I know we shouldn't have kept putting off telling her that she was adopted," Molly continued. "I understand that withholding that information made her susceptible in more ways than one. We just... We didn't want to upset her. We love her so much, you see. In all honesty, we forget that she's not ours biologically, that we're not a proper family—"

"You *are* a proper family. You're the real deal. Ally's a very lucky girl."

"I just want to make her life as amazing as it can possibly be."

"Don't try so hard." It's what Shelley had said to me. "There's great value in just letting things flow naturally."

"I… Maybe you're right. I want to put it all behind us and start afresh. Once again thank you for all you've done. I hear Angus's uncle's offer has been accepted, that it's all going through. Will he be starting work quite soon at the lighthouse?"

"Yes." And in the meantime the parents had drawn up a rota of daily visits and tasks to be performed, including the removal of more debris, a bit of scrubbing and cleaning, the liberal use of bleach… all with Uncle Glenn's delight and approval, who'd promised them the party of the year to look forward to on opening night.

The tower light couldn't stay on indefinitely, in fact, when Liam had tried to get it going the night after it wouldn't even flicker. No matter; it had done its job, as had he. The parents promised to leave a light of some description blazing come nightfall – it would never be allowed to reside in darkness again. Guardians of the lighthouse – they all were, more than thirteen in number, an army, and with Angus at the helm.

* * *

November had given way to December as I made my way to a remote woodland spot in the depths of East Sussex. The air was crisp, not bitter as it had been on Skye, dark clouds gathering above me and threatening yet another onslaught of rain. Parking my car where I'd parked it so often during the police investigation, I was relieved to see no one else mad enough to walk here on a day like today – only me. To be honest, I'm sure the fact that there was no one here had nothing to do with the weather, but everything to do with the girls who'd died, who'd been murdered here – the spirit of one still so traumatised that she lingered still, hiding behind a veil of mists that only she – and sometimes I – could see. Claire was her name, and, walking to where X no longer marked the spot, I called out.

"Claire, do you remember me? My name's Ness, I've been here several times before, to try and speak to you, to get you to come out of hiding. Claire," I continued, "you've nothing to fear from me. I've come here to help you leave this place behind and all the pain, and terror that you suffered here too. Your friend has left, and now it's your turn. Don't stay anymore, it's lonely here, go to where those who love you are waiting."

It was as I expected: no answer.

The man who did this to her, who trapped her in more ways than one, I was having trouble forgiving him too. How could he do this? How could anyone hurt a child? But people could, I knew that. I'd *seen* what they could do. There were plenty capable of committing such a heinous deed. Maybe they'd had terrible childhoods themselves, but even as I thought it, I dismissed it. There was no excuse. None. Everyone has a choice, two paths to follow. If you start walking down the wrong one...

"Claire, I'm not going to give up on you. I want to be clear about that. There's a light that shines, and I want you to go towards it; that's your home, where you belong. You'll be happier there, much happier, please believe me. I have a sense about that too."

A noise broke the silence – not a bird cawing, so few birds sing here, but the snap of a twig. I turned my head towards it, my eyes searching. Nothing. No one. Perhaps it was a rabbit or a fox or whatever animal calls the woods home, but in their case, quite rightly.

Hunkering down, I rubbed my hands over the ground, which is covered in leaves, small stones and clumps of mud. At once an earthy smell drifted upwards and I inhaled deeply. It smelled so good, so natural, no trace of the bodies that had once festered there. In spite of what happened, the seasons still change, the wind still blows, and the world still turns – life carries on. But I won't forget the dead. I'll be their champion. I'm on their side.

"Claire, I'm going to keep this simple. I'll come here on a regular basis, as often as I can. I won't force you to come forward, I can't. I don't have that power. Sometimes I'll sit and chat and you can perhaps listen. Other times I'll only spend a few minutes before I have to go. Take all the time you need. When you're ready, step forward and show yourself. That light I was talking about? I'll walk with you towards it; I'll go as far as I can with you. I hope that's sooner rather than later. You see, it's not good to be alone. It can make you… susceptible. I hope with me visiting regularly, you won't feel that way, you'll feel stronger. I'll say goodbye, Claire, for now."

I waited several more seconds, just in case, and then I retraced my footsteps, back to where I'd left my car. Closer to it, I heard another movement behind me, and turned.

"Claire?"

And if not her, could it be someone else, someone I longed to see – my mirror image? My heart raced at the thought.

"Is it you? Have you come back?"

If she had, she was silent too.

"I'm not ignoring you, not anymore. Why do you insist on ignoring me?"

She got her stubborn streak from Mum, I was sure of it. Maybe I had too.

"You wanted me to live for both of us, and I've been trying to do that, you know, getting out a bit more, having fun. I've been to the cinema a couple of times, to pubs and even a restaurant. My work's busy too – I've got a few more private cases in lately."

If she was there, she was giving as good as she'd got, by dishing up a bit of karma, but I wouldn't get angry with her – those days were gone.

"The thing is, despite all that, it's you I miss. It's been twelve years."

Still there was nothing.

"Okay, all right," I said, digging in my coat pocket for my car key and withdrawing it. As I did, I sighed. "Have it your way, but you can't sulk forever. And do you know why?"

Deliberately I paused, to let the atmosphere build, to let the mystery that would reel her in – *eventually* – deepen.

She always loved to play games, so where was the harm in playing one now?

"Because I know your name," I said. "I finally managed to find it out."

The End

Also by the author

Eve: A Christmas Ghost Story
(Psychic Surveys Prequel)

What do you do when a whole town is haunted?

In 1899, in the North Yorkshire market town of Thorpe Morton, a tragedy occurred; 59 people died at the market hall whilst celebrating Christmas Eve, many of them children. One hundred years on and the spirits of the deceased are restless still, 'haunting' the community, refusing to let them forget.

In 1999, psychic investigators Theo Lawson and Ness Patterson are called in to help, sensing immediately on arrival how weighed down the town is. Quickly they discover there's no safe haven. The past taints everything.

Hurtling towards the anniversary as well as a new millennium, their aim is to move the spirits on, to cleanse the atmosphere so everyone – the living and the dead – can start again. But the spirits prove resistant and soon Theo and Ness are caught up in battle, fighting against something that knows their deepest fears and can twist them in the most dangerous of ways.

They'll need all their courage to succeed and the help of a little girl too – a spirit who didn't die at the hall, who shouldn't even be there...

Psychic Surveys Book One:
The Haunting of Highdown Hall

"Good morning, Psychic Surveys. How can I help?"

The latest in a long line of psychically-gifted females, Ruby Davis can see through the veil that separates this world and the next, helping grounded souls to move towards the light - or 'home' as Ruby calls it. Not just a job for Ruby, it's a crusade and one she wants to bring to the High Street. Psychic Surveys is born.

Based in Lewes, East Sussex, Ruby and her team of freelance psychics have been kept busy of late. Specialising in domestic cases, their solid reputation is spreading - it's not just the dead that can rest in peace but the living too. All is threatened when Ruby receives a call from the irate new owner of Highdown Hall. Film star Cynthia Hart is still in residence, despite having died in 1958.

Winter deepens and so does the mystery surrounding Cynthia. She insists the devil is blocking her path to the light long after Psychic Surveys have 'disproved' it. Investigating her apparently unblemished background, Ruby is pulled further and further into Cynthia's world and the darkness that now inhabits it.

For the first time in her career, Ruby's deepest beliefs are challenged. Does evil truly exist? And if so, is it the most relentless force of all?

Psychic Surveys Book Two:
Rise to Me

"This isn't a ghost we're dealing with. If only it were that simple…"

Eighteen years ago, when psychic Ruby Davis was a child, her mother – also a psychic – suffered a nervous breakdown. Ruby was never told why. "It won't help you to know," the only answer ever given. Fast forward to the present and Ruby is earning a living from her gift, running a high street consultancy – Psychic Surveys – specialising in domestic spiritual clearance.

Boasting a strong track record, business is booming. Dealing with spirits has become routine but there is more to the paranormal than even Ruby can imagine. Someone – something – stalks her, terrifying but also strangely familiar. Hiding in the shadows, it is fast becoming bolder and the only way to fight it is for the past to be revealed – no matter what the danger.

When you can see the light, you can see the darkness too.

And sometimes the darkness can see you.

Psychic Surveys Book Three:
44 Gilmore Street

"We all have to face our demons at some point."

Psychic Surveys – specialists in domestic spiritual clearance – have never been busier. Although exhausted, Ruby is pleased. Her track record as well as her down-to-earth, no-nonsense approach inspires faith in the haunted, who willingly call on her high street consultancy when the supernatural takes hold.

But that's all about to change.

Two cases prove trying: 44 Gilmore Street, home to a particularly violent spirit, and the reincarnation case of Elisha Grey. When Gilmore Street attracts press attention, matters quickly deteriorate. Dubbed the 'New Enfield', the 'Ghost of Gilmore Street' inflames public imagination, but as Ruby and the team fail repeatedly to evict the entity, faith in them wavers.

Dealing with negative press, the strangeness surrounding Elisha, and a spirit that's becoming increasingly territorial, Ruby's at breaking point. So much is pushing her towards the abyss, not least her own past. It seems some demons just won't let go…

Psychic Surveys Book Four:
Old Cross Cottage

It's not wise to linger at the crossroads…

In a quiet Dorset Village, Old Cross Cottage has stood for centuries, overlooking the place where four roads meet. Marred by tragedy, it's had a series of residents, none of whom have stayed for long. Pink and pretty, with a thatched roof, it should be an ideal retreat, but as new owners Rachel and Mark Bell discover, it's anything but.

Ruby Davis hasn't quite told her partner the truth. She's promised Cash a holiday in the country but she's also promised the Bells that she'll investigate the unrest that haunts this ancient dwelling. Hoping to combine work and pleasure, she soon realises this is a far more complex case than she had ever imagined.

As events take a sinister turn, lives are in jeopardy. If the terrible secrets of Old Cross Cottage are ever to be unearthed, an entire village must dig up its past.

Blakemort
(A Psychic Surveys Companion Novella)

"That house, that damned house. Will it ever stop haunting me?"

After her parents' divorce, five-year old Corinna Greer moves into Blakemort with her mother and brother. Set on the edge of the village of Whitesmith, the only thing attractive about it is the rent. A 'sensitive', Corinna is aware from the start that something is wrong with the house. Very wrong.

Christmas is coming but at Blakemort that's not something to get excited about. A house that sits and broods, that calculates and considers, it's then that it lashes out - the attacks endured over five years becoming worse. There are also the spirits, some willing residents, others not. Amongst them a boy, a beautiful, spiteful boy...

Who are they? What do they want? And is Corinna right when she suspects it's not just the dead the house traps but the living too?

This Haunted World Book One:
The Venetian

Welcome to the asylum…

2015

Their troubled past behind them, married couple, Rob and Louise, visit Venice for the first time together, looking forward to a relaxing weekend. Not just a romantic destination, it's also the 'most haunted city in the world' and soon, Louise finds herself the focus of an entity she can't quite get to grips with – a 'veiled lady' who stalks her.

1938

After marrying young Venetian doctor, Enrico Sanuto, Charlotte moves from England to Venice, full of hope for the future. Home though is not in the city; it's on Poveglia, in the Venetian lagoon, where she is set to work in an asylum, tending to those that society shuns. As the true horror of her surroundings reveals itself, hope turns to dust.

From the labyrinthine alleys of Venice to the twisting, turning corridors of Poveglia, their fates intertwine. Vengeance only waits for so long…

This Haunted World Book Two:
The Eleventh Floor

A snowstorm, a highway, a lonely hotel…

Devastated by the deaths of her parents and disillusioned with life, Caroline Daynes is in America trying to connect with their memory. Travelling to her mother's hometown of Williamsfield in Pennsylvania, she is caught in a snowstorm and forced to stop at The Egress hotel – somewhere she'd planned to visit as her parents honeymooned there.

From the moment she sets foot inside the lobby and meets the surly receptionist, she realises this is a hotel like no other. Charming and unique, it seems lost in time with a whole cast of compelling characters sheltering behind closed doors.

As the storm deepens, so does the mystery of The Egress. Who are these people she's stranded with and what secrets do they hide? In a situation that's becoming increasingly nightmarish, is it possible to find solace?

Jessa*mine*

"The dead of night, Jess, I wish they'd leave me alone."

Jessamin Wade's husband is dead - a death she feels wholly responsible for. As a way of coping with her grief, she keeps him 'alive' in her imagination - talking to him everyday, laughing with him, remembering the good times they had together. She thinks she will 'hear' him better if she goes somewhere quieter, away from the hustle and bustle of her hometown, Brighton. Her destination is Glenelk in the Highlands of Scotland, a region her grandfather hailed from and the subject of a much-loved painting from her childhood.

Arriving in the village late at night, it is a bleak and forbidding place. However, the house she is renting - Skye Croft - is warm and welcoming. Quickly she meets the locals. Her landlord, Fionnlagh Maccaillin, is an ex-army man with obvious and not so obvious injuries. Maggie, who runs the village shop, is also an enigma, startling her with her strange 'insights'. But it is Stan she instantly connects with. Maccaillin's grandfather and a frail, old man, he is grief-stricken from the recent loss of his beloved Beth.

All four are caught in the past. All four are unable to let go. Their lives entwining in mysterious ways, can they help each other to move on or will they always belong to the ghosts that haunt them?

A note from the author

You can also subscribe to my newsletter to keep up-to-date with book releases, competitions and special offers http://eepurl.com/beoHLv or connect via my Facebook page – https://www.facebook.com/shani.struthers/ and Twitter – https://twitter.com/shani_struthers. Either way it'd be good to hear from you!

www.shanistruthers.com